PITIFUL LIES

JERSEY BAD BOYS
BOOK 3

C.D. GORRI

PITIFUL LIES

Jersey Bad Boys
Book 3
By C.D. Gorri

Copyright C.D. Gorri, NJ 2024

Before you begin sign up for my newsletter here:
SUBSCRIBE HERE

This is a work of fiction. All of the characters, names, places, organizations, and events portrayed in this novel are either part of the author's imagination and/or used fictitiously and are not to be construed as real. Any resemblance to any person, living or dead, actual events, locales or organizations is entirely coincidental. This eBook is licensed for your personal enjoyment only. All rights are reserved. No part of this book is to be reproduced, scanned, downloaded, printed, or distributed in any manner whatsoever without written permission from the author. Please do not participate in or encourage piracy of any materials in violation of the author's rights. Thank you for respecting the hard work of this author.

DEDICATION

They say the bigger they are the harder they fall. But when he's so determined to have you, he'll move heaven and earth to get you, being big and bad is a good thing. In fact, it's everything.

This book is dedicated to those of us who pass Captain America by so we can drool over the other guys. You know the ones. Frank Castle, Wolverine, Deadpool.

Yeah, those guys.

*So if you think that's you,
let me introduce you to Angel Fury.*

This one is for my editor, the incomparable Tammy

Payne, my Beta Readers, and my ARC team, you are each of you sensational and I adore you.

Thank you for helping me get these book babies, just right.

Oh, and Shelly? I didn't forget about you. Look for the meeting you asked for between the pages.

XOXO,
C.D.

JERSEY BAD BOYS

There's no room for mercy in a kingdom built on lies.

Beneath the veneer of polite society exists a criminal organization known for its utter lack of mercy. They call themselves the Vipers. The men who belong to this syndicate are cruel, cunning, and unforgiving. Ruled by a king, this band of brothers knows no boundaries and takes no prisoners. To cross them is to sign your own death certificate.

But even serpents have weaknesses.

And sometimes that weakness is just a flower.

Our Bad Boys:
Nico Fury
Luc Batiste
Angel Fury

Content Warnings:

This is a contemporary romance series of connected standalones, featuring familiar tropes such as enemies to lovers, forced proximity, arranged marriages, secret babies, and contains some violence, and explicit sex scenes. Profanity, graphic, steamy scenes, violence, homicide, talk of deceased relatives, references to sexual assault and abuse (not by the MCs), mention of domestic violence (not perpetrated by MCs), mention of suicide, alcohol consumption, misogyny (not the MCs), questionable morals, hurtful past, manipulations, fake relationships, lies, revenge, forced marriages, very bad decisions, and romantic obsessions that may be unhealthy, or toxic.

This is a fictional story with fictional characters. This is not real life.

*Always take care of your mental, emotional, and physical self because you are important.

PITIFUL LIES

Denial is just another type of lie. But sometimes it's all a girl has.

Giselle

Okay, so I threw a glass of beer in his face the first time I saw him. I thought he was his cousin and that he was treating my best friend badly.

It was an honest mistake. I didn't know the psycho was going to see it as a challenge and form a fixation on me. My answer was a firm, resounding *no*.

But that didn't seem to stop him. And when a group of drunk guys decided to follow me home one night after I left the Den, I had to admit, it paid to have a stalker who was six foot six inches of pure, tattooed muscle.

Angel Fury was something to behold, and now that he made it into my bed, I was afraid he'd slithered into other places. Like my heart. There was only one way to get rid of the man who would only cause me pain in the end.

Deny. Deny. Deny.

Angel

The first time I saw Giselle Vega, I knew I wanted her. The curvy goddess stood toe to toe with a monster like me and didn't even bat an eyelash. It wasn't every day I met a woman feisty enough to take me on.

She could keep spouting her pitiful lies, but I knew the truth. I felt it every time I touched her. She was crazy about me. And I wanted to keep her. I just had to get her addicted. So, I decided to lay in wait, like the Viper I was.

That was the thing about snakes. Sure, we hibernated at times, but we always struck when least expected.

My pretty Little Doll has no idea what was coming for her.

Pitiful Lies is the third in the contemporary romance series of connected standalones, Jersey Bad Boys. This series features familiar tropes such as enemies to lovers, forced proximity, arranged marriages, secret babies, and contains some violence and explicit scenes.

JERSEY BAD BOYS

PROLOGUE ONE-ANGEL

Early Summer

Anticipation is something a lot of guys discount, but it's kept me alive for forty-two years.

Some people think a lifestyle like mine is part act, and they aren't wrong. There is something to say about being the Enforcer to the most powerful criminal organization in town and showmanship.

But if this is an act, then I am always *on*.

I don't wear a costume. All of this is me. And it is real.

My height.
My bulk.
My ink.
The metal in my ears.

And the weapons strategically concealed around my body.

I sit in the shadows, a tightly coiled serpent, waiting to strike at anyone who comes into my house with ill intent.

The Vipers' Den is our place.

It is dark and loud. A little pretentious, and one of the most sought after night spots in the tri-state.

A nightclub and bar, it's the perfect cover for a syndicate like ours. Nico, Luc, and I run the Vipers, and this is our base of operations.

We each have offices in the basement, and like any good snake pit there are hallways and secret passages that serve our needs well.

We run a tight organization with Nico as our king. He's my real cousin, but me, him, and Luc are all blood brothers. We've each put in enough blood, sweat, and tears to make this thing ours.

I don't mind having a king. A snake needs one head to lead, and Nico is perfect for the job. Luc is all brains, and his team of lawyers keeps us solid. I'm the guy in charge of all security, and I've spent the last few weeks increasing our fucking numbers.

This feeling I have, it's been building. I don't know what it is, but something is happening.

The atmosphere is ripe with expectation.

Like some shit is about to go down.

But I'm ready. I am always ready. I have to be.

The DJ is spinning some shit with a heavy bass, but I'm not really paying attention to the song.

Things are getting tense. But Nico's mind isn't where it should be.

Oh, I know where it is. Ever since I brought that cute little baker girl here to clear her brother's debts, a part of him has been MIA.

It's none of my fucking business. Nobody else's, either.

Nico, Luc, and I built this thing up from the ground when we were still wet behind the ears.

Nico is the king because he fucking earned it.

I don't want the crown.

I never did.

I am happy right where I am. Doing what I do best. Cracking skulls and putting the fear of God in those who are too stupid to know they shouldn't fuck with us.

The Vipers are feared and respected. We are the gatekeepers. We control the ports and that means money and power. Never mind the cops, businessmen, and politicians we have in our pockets.

The thing is, when you have assets like that,

there's always some asshole wanting to test you. And with Nico otherwise occupied, it's on me to make sure no one gets through our defenses.

I'm the Enforcer.

The guys who work under me are all muscle, and they are loyal to the organization. I see to all our security needs, and I make sure anyone needing a lesson gets it.

Luc is the Council.

A bonafide fucking Princeton grad and a lawyer to boot. He handles all the business deals and makes sure our legit side is where it needs to be.

As for my cousin, Nico?

Well, like I said, he's the undisputed King of the Vipers. That means he does a little bit of everything.

Nico is unhinged in the best possible way. He is cunning and sharp as a tack. I'm proud of the fucker.

I started working with him and Luc when they were just teenagers, and I was barely twenty. A bad batch of heroin sent Nico's mother and Luc's sister to their graves far too fucking early.

That skinny brainiac and my hotheaded cousin took on the local dealers themselves and almost wound up dead for their efforts.

That's where I came in. I started out as an

amateur MMA fighter, but I switched from main event type shit to underground matches.

When I got a hold of Nico and Luc, all black and blue from a beating they took, I decided to teach them a thing or two about fighting.

So, at my core, that's what I am.

A fighter.

The three of us together were harder to defeat than any of the old gangs wanted to admit.

But look at us now.

We are the Vipers.

And no one crosses us and lives to tell the tale.

So, when the king is busy, I watch over the Den. Here I sit, minding the king's throne and making sure everyone knows who and what we are.

A group of scantily clad women sashays past me, and I give them a once over.

It's what they want. What they expect. And I am a man who appreciates beauty.

They're too obvious for my tastes, though. I'm forty-two, not twenty-five. Spandex and stilettos aren't what I look for in female companionship these days.

But then something, or rather, someone, catches my eye. She's about five foot four inches tall and about a buck eighty, by my estimation.

That might be large to some guys, but not to me.

I'm six foot six inches tall and I am easily twice the curvy little woman's weight.

My cock starts to twitch behind my slacks as I take in her purposeful stride.

Little Doll is walking right towards me, I realize and raise my eyes to her face.

Holy fuck.

If looks could kill I'd be dead on all accounts.

The woman is, well, there's no other word for it, stunning.

She is stunning.

Thick, dark tendrils of curls spiral down her back, past her shoulders, in a wild mane that bounces when she walks.

I want to see it spread across my pillow like some dark dream. I bet it will look sexy as fuck.

I adjust my thickening cock and sit forward, placing my full frosted beer mug on the table at my side.

Her hips switch as she walks, bringing attention to the indent of her waist. My eyes travel down her body. I moan at the sight of her cleavage. Her big tits jiggle with every move, and that is not even the best part.

Lower still, my gaze rakes over her covetously,

stopping once I get to the little skirt she has on with two slits on either side.

Holy. Fuck.

Little Doll has got a set of legs on her.

Oofah.

Every time she steps, a flash of pale skin shows her thick fucking thighs as she walks.

I want to feel those thighs wrapped around my head while I feast on her dripping cunt.

I lick my lips, my gaze going back to her sweetheart of a face.

But she ain't smiling at me. In fact, her pale green eyes are flashing with an emotion I register as anger.

Like white hot fucking anger.

She is closer now, and I gotta admit I'm more than a little curious.

I mean, I don't know this woman from Eve.

But I want to.

And I want to know why she's pissed.

Of course, I wasn't expecting her to grab my mug of beer and toss the contents in my face.

"You bastard! Are you really just sitting here looking for your next fuck after you knock my friend up!" she yells, and I'm soaked, but I don't even blink.

How can I when she looks so fucking divine in all her fury?

But that's my name. And I'm about to show her what it means.

PROLOGUE TWO-GISELLE

So, this whole shitshow that is my life all started when I tossed a mug of beer in Angel Fury's sexy as hell face.

Of course, the enormous fucker just sat there after I did it, freezing me in place with his icy blue eyes.

Jesus. Christ.

Those eyes of his were like nothing I have ever seen. And for a split second, I hated myself for wanting the man my best friend was hung up on.

At the time, I had mistaken him for his cousin.

Anyway, after about a second, he stood up, towering over me. After his eyes and his bulk, the next thing I noticed were his tattoos.

He was inked up from head to toe, it seemed. And I liked it. I liked it a lot.

He stunned me, grabbing me by my waist and slamming his mouth against mine in some kind of barbaric claim.

I was shocked to say the least.

And turned on. Very, very turned on.

And that was something that completely horrified me. But I had to admit, I didn't push him away. I kissed him back.

The first thing I tasted was beer. Likely the one I'd tossed at him. The second thing was him.

Masculine power and mint.

Not realizing he wasn't the father of Anna's baby, I did the only thing I could do in self-defense.

I slapped him.

But that only made him smile, and the second I saw that expression, I was done for.

"I don't know what it is you think I did, Koukla, But I promise I'll fix it," he said, then he kissed me again.

"Wait," I gasped, and turned my head, trying to catch my breath.

"What about Anna?" I asked.

"Anna? Who's Anna?" he replied, and my mouth dropped open.

"Aren't you Nico Fury?" I asked.

"Nah, Little Doll. I'm his cousin. Angel. Angel Fury," he said, still not letting go of me.

"Oh shit," I murmured, realizing my grievous mistake.

"Yeah, oh shit. You disrespected me in front of an audience, Koukla. Now you have to make it up to me," he growled into my ear.

Knowing who and what the Vipers were, I nodded my head. I didn't need that kind of trouble in my life.

I said *no* the first few times. But then, well, I agreed. And yeah, I went out with him.

Well. Not *out* out. Just to the Den.

I did it so he could save face. I played the part, acting like the big bad Viper's girlfriend.

It was easy at first. Falling into bed with Angel was downright enjoyable.

The best I ever had.

While Anna and Maria were finding their happy-ever-afters, I was dreaming about mine.

But I'm not lucky like them.

Angel isn't like Nico or Luc. He's not anything like his namesake.

No. The big, sexy man is a devil in disguise.

Still, I didn't expect him to break my heart. But

that's my fault. I believed he wanted me as much as I wanted him.

I have to be honest, though. Angel made no promises or declarations. And after seeing him in the Den with a skinny blonde perched on his lap, I didn't need any.

I dated cheaters before, and it never ended well for me. I wouldn't do it again.

So, I ran.

I took the easy way out.

I skipped town when my best friend was about to have a baby, and I did it for the most cowardly reason of all.

Because my feelings were hurt.

Pitiful, right?

Fuck.

I am not usually such a wimp, but I just couldn't face a lying, cheating bastard like Angel Fury.

Anna and Maria will forgive me. That's what best friends do.

I just need some time to myself. Away from my mess. Time to heal and forget whatever that was I allowed to happen between us.

The fact is, it's over now. I have to move on. I *will* move on.

Because I'm a motherfucking badass, and Angel Fury is nothing to me.

Liar.

I wince as the word enters my brain and I force it out just as quickly as it snuck in.

I can get over this, *over him*, I know I can.

It's just a matter of time.

PROLOGUE THREE-GISELLE

Almost two months later.

I close my phone after checking out the newest images of Nico Jr. that Anna just sent over and I will myself not to cry.

Fuck.

Everything is so fucked up. I don't know what to do anymore.

I know it's stupid and weak, but after seeing Angel with that beautiful blonde stranger plastered all over him, I couldn't just stick around.

I had to leave town.

For weeks, Angel made me believe we were an item.

The real deal.

Sure, it all happened unconventionally. I mean, I

did toss a beer in his face, and he did kinda force me to play his girlfriend.

But somewhere the lines got blurred. I went from acting a part to believing it.

Maybe it was when he bent me over the sofa in his office, lifted my skirt, and fucked me from behind like a man on a mission.

Or it could have been when he drove me home later and cupped my face tenderly, kissing me until I damn near melted into a puddle of goo.

There was no audience either time.

Just us.

After that, our fake-relationship seemed pretty not-fake to me.

Angel seemed to like my super curvy and ultra thick body. And I sure as fuck liked his giant-sized muscular one.

Angel Fury is simply too hot for his own good. His face is perfection. Sometimes, it hurts to look at him.

The asshole.

His eyes are more aquamarine than sapphire blue, and I love them. Sometimes, they look almost white.

Ethereal.

Gorgeous.

Fantastic.

His cheekbones and powerful jaw are almost too masculine, but it's all softened by sinfully delicious lips.

Seriously, I just wanna sit on his face for like hours with those things.

I have.

Which makes this so fucking hard. I wish I hadn't tried to surprise him. I wish I didn't know about her. The other woman.

But I do know. And it's killing me.

It only emphasizes how little about the man I actually bothered to learn during our tryst.

Angel isn't what I would call a *sharer*. I've never even seen his house.

Yes, we hung out.

Usually at the Vipers' Den.

Yes, we fucked like bunnies.

Again, usually in his office, which, for obvious reasons, sported a huge bedroom.

But we rarely talked. And we didn't do other things normal couples did.

We didn't date. Or go out to dinner. Or meet each other's families. Or, well, anything, really.

"Did you pick a color?" the manicurist interrupts

my spiraling thoughts, and I hand her the hot pink I chose for my mani-pedi.

"Okay, this way. Would you like me to turn on the chair massage?"

"Oh God, fuck yes. Oops! Sorry, I meant to say, yes, please," I tell her, and she smiles and nods knowingly.

She turns on the water and fills the foot tub, adding a blue tablet. I sit back in the chair and close my eyes, humming low in my throat as I try to ease away the horrible month I've had with a little self-care.

Missing all these milestones in Anna's life makes me feel like a total asshole. She and Nico bought a house in the suburbs and Jr. is just on his way to take over the world already. Maria and Luc got hitched, too.

I am missing it all.

Just because I am a pitiful coward.

FML.

"Would you like a real massage? Your shoulders look tense," the same manicurist asks.

"Sure," I reply.

My eyes are still closed as I lean forward to give her room. It's Fort Lauderdale and hot as fuck even in September.

I'm wearing a cami and a pair of booty shorts. Just like everyone else. But I still feel overheated.

Big, warm hands clasp my skin and start massaging. And my eyes fly wide open.

I know those hands.

Oh no. How the fuck did he find me here?

"Don't touch me."

I say it even though I want his hands on me. And the realization makes me mad.

I look right into Angel's pale blue eyes, and I frown, hard.

Fuck him for coming here, looking better than anyone has a right to. And who does he think he is massaging my shoulders?

I try to move, but he holds me firmly in place.

"Don't touch you, Koukla? You sure? Last time I saw you, you were begging for my touch. Remember?"

His words have me squeezing my thighs together. I'm already so turned on, just one touch and I'd likely combust.

"That was before I knew you're nothing but a two-timing cheat," I reply between clenched teeth and try to shake him off.

But Angel is impossible to move. And his eyes narrow like he is super pissed.

"I think we got ourselves a misunderstanding here. But no worries. We'll get that all straightened out on the way back home," he says, standing to his full height.

And it is impressive. Bastard just has to be tall, dark, tattooed, and handsome as the goddamn devil himself.

Fuck him twice for that.

"What are you talking about? I'm not going anywhere with you."

"Little Doll, you can come quietly, or you can scream. Your choice," he pauses, pressing his mouth against my ear. "You know how much I like it when you scream."

Then he licks my neck, biting down hard, before backing up and handing the manicurist a couple of hundreds.

"Don't worry about your parents. I got your suitcase from your mother. She's a very nice lady. Says she's been wondering why you haven't left to see Anna. Your father, too."

"You went to my parents' condo?" I ask, eyes wide.

"Yep. Hey, you think you can work fast?"

"Yes, sir," the manicurist says.

"Cool. Thanks. You, uh, want me to keep

massaging those shoulders, Gorgeous? Or anything else? I'm always available for you," he says to me.

This prick.

"No thanks. You're not needed here," I say, arching one eyebrow.

I grab the remote for the chair and press the button to start the deluxe message.

Fuck this asshole.

I ignore him for the next twenty minutes. And yeah, I'm bouncing around the goddamn massage chair while my toenails are being polished, and I am waiting for him to walk away so I can text Anna or Maria, anyone who will sympathize with me.

But he just stands there. Watching me.

Stupid cheating jerk.

I try to close my eyes to block him out.

Two-timing shithead.

I fucking earned this pedicure and I'm going to goddamn enjoy it

Even if I look like a bag of Jello while the bulky massage chair does its thing.

PROLOGUE FOUR-ANGEL

I'm not made for serious relationships, but something about this woman won't let me leave her alone.

Giselle Vega.

The one who ran away.

Literally.

I call her Koukla. It means *beautiful doll* or *little doll*, which is how I think of Giselle.

She's short. And she's beautiful.

Hauntingly so.

She's got this body that just won't quit. And her mouth. Her fucking mouth drives me insane.

We were messing around for a little while, and I thought we were good.

But something happened, and I don't know what.

Giselle ran, and I tried to stay away.

Really, I did.

I'm not the kinda guy who chases women. But I am chasing her. I just can't help it.

I watch my Little Doll bouncing around in that massage chair and it's all I can do not to toss her over my shoulder.

I'm still not ruling that out yet.

She can spout all the pitiful lies she wants about not needing me or wanting me. But I feel something every time we're near one another.

And she feels it too.

Whether or not she wants to admit it.

Seven weeks, almost two months, that's how long she's been gone. It isn't a very long time, but it sure feels like it.

My concentration has been shit. Days seem longer, lonelier, too. But maybe that's from one too many sleepless nights just thinking about where Giselle is and who she's with.

Why'd you run, Koukla? Is it someone else?

I fucking hate thinking about her with another man. Even picturing her talking to one makes me want to commit homicide.

Makes me goddamn rabid.

Anna is helpful with that part. She tells me where

she's gone before I can track her myself.

When Anna left Nico, he made the executive decision to try to stay out of her life. He didn't want his darkness poisoning her light.

Whatever. They still ended up together. Just spent six months apart, and I know my cousin regrets that.

As for me? I'm not that good a person. Trusting her to realize her mistake on her own, to miss me—*or even her friends, though it pains me to say that*—enough to want to come back.

I sit and wait, but it's been almost two months. And this has gone on long enough.

I know she's been with her family. And yeah, I've had eyes on her. Sent a few of my team down there to keep watch.

So fucking what?

It might be creepy having someone tail her, but I'm okay with a little creeping.

I had to know she was safe and sound for my own peace of mind.

Only, it hasn't been peaceful since she left. I have not had one decent night's sleep in all this time.

It's like I got this hole in me since she's been gone. An ever-growing ache only she can soothe.

But now she's in my sights. And that pain I've been feeling? Well, it's finally subsiding.

Just like I knew it would.

The massage chair finally stops, and Giselle opens her eyes. My breath stalls. Fuck, she is stunning. That celery green gaze I've missed so much catches mine, and I'm already hard for her.

I've never seen eyes that color. With her almost black hair and her sun kissed skin, she looks like something out of a wet dream. Mine, mainly.

"Ready, Koukla?" I ask, my voice coming out grittier than I intended.

But I don't wait for an answer. I just bend down and grab her by the waist. She's so tiny, my hands are almost the size of her torso.

"What are you doing?" she asks on a whisper.

I don't answer. I simply pick her up. I drop a hard kiss on her mouth, stopping her fidgeting, then I toss my sweet cinnamon smelling Koukla over my shoulder. Just like a sack of potatoes.

A sexy sack of potatoes.

"Angel!" she yells and hits my back.

It's cute.

"Knock it off, Little Doll, or I'll be forced to punish you. And if I do that, this ride is gonna be a lot messier than you want," I say and spank her juicy ass, giving it a squeeze before moving my hand to the inside of her thigh.

Heat from her pussy sears me, and I bite back my groan. She stills immediately and I don't bother to hide my smirk.

She can't see it anyway.

"If you don't put me down, Angel, I swear to God I am going to kill you," she hisses.

A chuckle spills from my lips. There she is.

Goddamn.

I missed that mouth.

This is gonna be so much fun.

CHAPTER ONE-ANGEL

Giselle is facing the window, refusing to look at me, and it's annoying. I know we have to talk, but how can I start if she won't acknowledge I'm there?

Curiosity wars with pure animal lust every time I glance her way. Truly, I don't get it.

Me and Sisi always had a good time together. I mean, *I know* she had a good time whenever we were in the bedroom in my office, fucking each other's brains out.

My Little Doll is vocal. She lets me know when she likes what I am doing to her body. It's one of the hottest things about her.

And let me tell you, she likes what I do to her body.

"Why did you leave?" I ask, breaking the silence.

Giselle turns her head and gives me a dirty look. But she doesn't answer.

Now, I'm getting more than annoyed. I'm getting pissed.

"Fine. We'll do it your way," I murmur, too low for her to hear me.

I bite the inside of my cheek as I drive the rest of the way to the private airport where the Viper Enterprises' jet sits waiting for me in silence.

Little Doll still hasn't turned towards me. She has her arms crossed. Probably cold. I am guessing due to the fact she is wearing a pitiful little excuse for a shirt.

I adjust the temperature. When I look at her again, she is biting her bottom lip.

Fuck. I want to be the one who does that.

I get a good look at her outfit once more and I narrow my eyes. She went out like that?

How many times? Who's seen my Koukla dressed like this?

Her clothes are barely existent. I get it. We're in Florida.

But what the fuck?

I'm going to have to have a talk with her about that. The spaghetti straps look like they might pop, freeing those big, gorgeous tits, and I am beside myself with anticipation and raging jealousy that someone else might see.

I can't help myself, though. The temptation is too great. But even though I hit one or two potholes on purpose, the material holds out, much to my chagrin.

That's alright.

I'll have her back in my bed where she belongs in no time. I don't know where Giselle got the idea I'm interested in other women, but I'm not.

How could I be? She is more than enough for me.

No, I never cheated on her. Not in thought or action. And yeah, it pisses me off she thinks that of me.

But when I think about it, it's my fault. Really, what kind of impression have I made on this girl?

She must think I'm some kind of mindless rutting jackass. Every time I am near her, all I can think about is sticking my dick inside her tight, wet pussy.

What can I say?

We've got animal magnetism going for us if nothing else. But nah, that's just me being a smartass.

There is something else. Something I never felt before, but I'll be damned if I tell her first.

I pull into an empty spot just as she sits forward. The sun is baking me through the windows the second I turn the engine off.

"Where are we?" she asks, sitting forward and I frown, noting the way the tank top dips, and her nipples almost spill out.

If I can see her, so can my guys standing around outside while I pull into a spot.

"Sit back, Koukla," I tell her, and she frowns, but complies.

"What?"

I nod towards her top, and she looks down. Her cheeks burn pink, but she complies and sits back.

"What does that mean, anyway? For months now, you've been calling me *Koukla*. And for all I know, it could mean fat ass," she snarks.

"It don't mean fat ass," I reply, and my lip twitches.

But I don't smile. Not yet.

"Wait for me to come around," I command.

"Fine. Neanderthal," she mutters.

That time I do smile, but I wait until I'm outside the car, so Giselle doesn't see it.

"Hey yo, Boss?" Bernard, a new guy, walks up to me, his eyes on the passenger window.

I move in front of him, forcing him to stop short

and blocking his view of my girl. I don't care if she's in denial or what.

Little Doll is mine.

And I don't have no loyalty to this motherfucker here. Especially not if he's too stupid to live.

"Got a problem?" I snarl.

"Um, yeah, no, Boss," he says, hands raised.

"What do you want?" I ask this imbecile.

"Oh, uh, so the plane needs servicing. Pilot says it's gonna be a couple of hours."

"What? Fine. Fuck that. You guys wait and fly back home."

"What about you, Boss?" he asks, but I'm already walking back to the driver's side.

"Don't fucking ask questions, Bernard," Anthony, one of my old time guys, says to him.

I nod at Anthony, but I don't bother replying. When I give orders, I expect them to be followed.

If Bernard can't deal with that, he knows what to do. And if he doesn't, well, Anthony will show him.

"What's happening?" Giselle asks, and her green eyes are so wide I want to groan.

The color is so light, and the green is unlike anything I ever saw. Eyes like hers are rare. Perfect.

They're not emeralds.

They're peridots.

It's this stone I saw once that's a mix of yellow and green. Like celery, for lack of a better comparison.

Koukla has eyes like that. Cat eyes. And they are just as gorgeous as the rest of her.

"Change of plans. We're driving back."

I turn the engine on with the push of a button and adjust the controls so we ride in comfort. I reach behind her seat and find one of my sweatshirts, and I hold it out to her.

"What? I am not sitting in a car with you for twenty hours, Angel," she says, and my blood hums at the sound of my name on her mouth.

Next time she says it, she'll be screaming it.

That's a promise I make to myself.

"Take the sweatshirt. And don't worry, I have an impeccable driving record," I say, pretending that's what her objection is about.

"Yeah, right. I've seen you drive, buddy," she mutters, but I notice she's checking her seatbelt.

For a moment, I thought maybe she would try to fight me on this or jump out. But Giselle is not stupid.

Jumping out of a car, even if it's only doing twenty-five miles per hour, is a pretty risky move.

Just in case, though, I lock the doors.

"Pull over at the next gas station. I'll Uber back to my parents' condo," she says.

"I don't think so."

I snicker out loud. This girl is so damn feisty with me. Like she doesn't care that I'm more than twice her size with a reputation that would intimidate most grown men.

It should annoy me, but it doesn't. When Giselle gets all mouthy with me, hell, it just turns me on all the more.

I want her.

I mean that. I want this woman in a completely obsessive way.

I always fucking want her.

And that's, *well*, that's new.

That's the real reason I can't just forget about her. I can't just let her go. Can't watch her walk out on me.

Not gonna happen.

I mean, I fucking tried. Maybe I'm just too old. Or too jaded. Or just too damn fucking mean to leave this woman alone.

I'm not good for her.

I know I'm not.

Ask anyone what the name Angel Fury means, and they'll tell you the same thing.

It means death.

Yeah, I got blood on my hands. A lot of it. I'm a motherfucking Viper. I am the Enforcer.

No one walks away from me and survives. Now, that never applied to women before, but Giselle isn't some one night stand.

She isn't one of those women who knows the rules. You know the ones I mean. The hard ones. Like groupies, only I ain't a fucking rock star. I am something else.

Something darker. Forbidden. Something certain women want to use to scratch an itch when they're tired of their staid lives.

But Giselle's not like that. She's a breath of fresh air. No guile, just stark honesty and she's so in your fucking face. And yet she is still so complex. Like she has secrets and I'm dying to know what they are.

I fucking love that about her. She makes me want to dive deep, discover it all. And I will. Even if she fights me the whole time.

A sick part of me hopes she does. But another side of me, the tender one I don't acknowledge very often, wants her to surrender willingly.

It wants her to trust me.

Fuck, what has she done to me? Since when do I care if a woman trusts me?

Never before. Only with her. Only right now.

This woman is not some piece of ass you can use and cast aside. She demands more. That's why I tracked her gorgeous ass all the way down to the Sunshine State.

Two months apart is all I can take. It's been long enough. I'm taking her back home.

Where she belongs.

Period. And no, I'm not going to look too closely at that, either.

"I am not driving all the way back to Jersey City with you."

"Yes, you are, Koukla. Be quiet now and let me drive, or else," I warn her.

"Or else what?" she snaps.

"Or else I'll find something to stick in that mouth to make you quiet."

She squeaks and turns her head to face the road. I want to laugh, but I quickly realize I'm an idiot because now all I can picture is her on her knees with my dick in her mouth.

I adjust my hard as fuck cock in my pants and I step on the gas pedal.

It's gonna be a very long ride.

CHAPTER TWO-GISELLE

B*astard.*
I can't believe Angel said that. Well, that's not exactly true.

Of course, I can believe it.

Angel is a big, sexy, tattooed giant who loves talking dirty.

It's one of the things I like most about him. Something I never thought I would ever admit to.

If only he wasn't talking to every woman he fucking looks at like that.

Sadness and lust war within me, but the cell phone in my pocket buzzes and I heave out a sigh.

"Whose texting you like that?" Angel asks, his thick black brows furrowed like he's curious, bordering on annoyed.

But I don't have it in me to play games with him. I'm not like that.

"It's my mom."

"Oh," he replies. "Call her."

"No," I tell him, and give him a look that says he's crazy.

"Koukla, call your mother. She might be worried about you."

We've been driving for four hours, but we haven't even made it to the top of Florida yet. This state just seems to go on forever, and I95 isn't even packed yet.

"And tell her what? That some lunatic kidnapped me from the nail salon?"

Angel sighs and just shakes his head. Before I can ask him what he's doing, he's pressing a button on the complicated-looking steering wheel of the insanely hot muscle car he's driving.

Then, he dials a familiar number. I can see it on the enormous monitor.

Oh my God.

It's my parents' number.

"How the fuck did you get—"

But I can't finish that question because my mother's voice greets me over the speakers.

"Is that you, Angel? Honey, an Angel is calling me on my phone," she says with laughter lacing her voice.

I think she's talking out loud maybe to my dad, but then again, she talks to herself whether or not he is there sometimes. My mom is fun like that.

I am too stunned to speak, but it appears I don't have to. Angel does it for me.

"Hello, Mrs. Vega," he says, and he's smiling.

Like, he's really fucking smiling.

I don't think I've ever seen him do that before. My heart constricts. It feels so full and tight all at the same time. A flurry of emotions hits me.

Sadness, regret, and a sort of mourning fills me. A requiem for lost dreams.

There's more, too. I don't know what it is exactly.

Maybe hope.

But that's idiotic, and I quickly douse that ember of feeling before it can become something else.

Something deadly.

You are so fucking pitiful, Sisi. You know that?

But I ignore my bitch of an inner voice, and I tune into the conversation between my cheating ex whatever and my mother.

"Now, what did I tell you before? If my handsome new almost son-in-law is going to call me anything, it's going to be Mom," she says in a sing-song voice.

"What?" I gasp before Angel can answer.

He's grinning at me now, and I want to hit him.

"Mom, he's not gonna call you that! *What did you do?*" I shout and mouth the last part to him.

But he doesn't bother answering me. Of course, he doesn't.

Fucker.

"Sisi, are you back in Jersey? I want you to check on Resa, she's been having trouble with her RA at school," she says.

"Okay, Mom, I will call her. But we're not in Jersey yet."

"What? Why not?" Mom asks.

"Sorry, that's my fault," Angel says. "I thought a tour of the coast might be nice. But don't you worry, Mrs. Vega, I'm a good driver."

"Oh, a road trip. How romantic! And I'm sure you are a very good driver, Angel. I know you'll take care of our baby. And if you won't call me Mom, I insist you call me Delia, okay?"

"Oh my God! Mom, what are you doing?"

"What am I doing? Oh, you mean talking to your fiancé, even though you never told me you had one? Really, Sisi, Daddy and I are kind of miffed about that. He's at the golf club now, but he is expecting a phone call from you later, young lady."

"What? I am not engaged—" I try to explain.

"Oh, I gotta go. That's the doorbell. Bye, kids. Call us later!"

Mom hangs up before I can correct her gross misinterpretation of mine and Angel's relationship.

This prick.

How could he do this to me? I mean lying to my parents about a relationship is one thing, but saying we are engaged? It just cuts way too close to the real issue. And that's that Angel is not serious about me at all.

And I want him to be. Isn't that the real problem?

I turn my body to face him, and he's not even looking at me. I am so mad right now, I could scream.

But I don't want him to crash, so instead, I settle for pinching him on the bicep. It's difficult since he has zero body fat, but I get a nice piece of skin between my nails, and I turn it hard.

"Ouch! What the hell, Koukla?"

"First of all, I call bullshit. You don't even have any fat for me to pinch," I grumble, and I know I am being ridiculous, but whatever.

"Yeah, well, pinching skin hurts, too," he replies, rubbing the spot, and I am momentarily mollified.

"Damn, if you want to get kinky with me, you

just gotta ask, Little Doll," he says, turning it into a joke.

And I am mad all over again.

"Why did you tell my parents we're engaged?" I cut to the chase.

"Don't be dumb, Sisi," he says.

I huff, crossing my arms and waiting for more of an explanation. Angel's cerulean gaze flashes at me before he exhales and nods his head.

"Be reasonable, Koukla. How else was I supposed to get your mother to give me your suitcase? I couldn't just say *Hey, Mrs. Vega, Can I have your daughter's things? We like to fuck sometimes, so I know she won't mind.* Somehow, I don't think that would have gone over very well."

Asshole.

Of course, he is right. But what the heck kind of explanation is that, anyway?

"First off, we are not fuck buddies," I tell him angry at his description of our former relationship.

We like to fuck sometimes.

I mean, even if that's true, fuck him for saying it so nonchalantly.

But before I can really give him a piece of my mind, Angel interrupts me.

"Finally, something we agree on, Koukla. Now, you want burgers or BBQ for lunch?"

"What?"

Is this guy serious?

How the hell can he just jump from discussing our past sexy times to food with no transition at all?

"Lunch, Sisi. What do you want to eat?"

"I'm not hungry," I reply, but my stomach growls, and he just gives me a *duh* look.

"Fine. I don't care. Either," I say.

Now I'm pissed off and hungry.

"Giselle," he says my full name, and it's like a command.

I swear I feel it all the way to my core. But I refuse to give Angel that kind of power, so I ignore the feeling and continue with my mulish behavior. Crossing my arms, I shrug.

"I really don't care," I say.

Now, he pulls over to the shoulder. His unwavering stare on my face. I try to hold out. I really do.

But three minutes of that stare is all I can stand.

"Fine! BBQ," I grumble, and he grins.

The prick.

"Good Girl," Angel praises me for answering him, and again, my core twitches with need.

CHAPTER THREE-GISELLE

This man is completely out of my realm of experience. He is over the top in ways I have no idea what to do with. But there is one thing I can't lie to myself about, and that is the fact that I still want him.

God help me, I really do.

"Wait for me," he says after pulling into an empty spot outside what looks like an honest to God shack in Jacksonville.

Yah, we are still in fucking Florida. This state just never ends.

There's a statue of a pink piglet outside of the wooden structure that looks like it will fall down if a strong wind hits it the right way.

The pig is cute, wearing an apron with a spatula

in his hand, but I can't help but think it's a little morbid considering he's cooking a rack of spareribs.

The delicious scent of smoky barbecue reaches my nostrils and my stomach growls again just as Angel opens the passenger door.

"Let's get you fed, Little Doll."

He holds out his inked up hand to me, and I take it, trying to ignore the sizzle that shoots up my spine from the seemingly platonic touch.

Of course, his words have a different meaning. I recall him saying the same thing once, but he was talking about feeding his dick to my pussy.

I squeeze my thighs together and clear my throat when I catch him watching me. I might be a lot of things, but one thing I am not is a good liar.

Angel smirks, and it's like that bastard can feel my need for him. I pull my hand from his grip and walk ahead of him to the window so I can order my own lunch.

After I am done telling the cashier what I want, I go to pay, but Angel slaps a credit card down before I can.

How I didn't feel his presence looming behind me, I don't know.

"Triple that order, pal, and put it on this," Angel says, and his voice sounds deep and serious.

Maybe even annoyed. I grin to myself. It's a small victory, but I'll take it.

I walk away from where Angel is still waiting for his credit card and find a table close by so we can hear when the food is ready.

His pale blue eyes look hard as he takes the seat across from me.

"I'm only going to say this once, Sisi. When you're with me, I pay, understand?"

Ooh.

I guess I hit a nerve. And I'm not going to pretend I don't like seeing him riled up, because I do.

So, I narrow my eyes, and I reach into my pocket, pulling out a twenty. I drop it on the table.

"Hate to break it to you, but I have a job, and I have my own money. I don't need any man to pay my way. Especially not one I'm through with," I tell him.

Angel leans over the table, and I swear his chest is rumbling like he's some kind of wild animal.

My breath hitches in my throat as he takes my chin in hand, forcing my eyes to remain on his.

I feel hunted.

Stalked.

And the moisture in my panties is telling me it's

not all bad being the object of a man's attention. That man in particular.

But I can't give in. I won't. Angel is a player and I'm through with getting my heart stomped on.

So, I grit my jaw and refuse to take the bait.

"Let's get one thing straight, Koukla. I'm not *any man*. I'm Angel fucking Fury and we ain't through until I say so, Little Doll."

He picks up the twenty and looks down my body before stuffing it back in my pocket with his free hand. I hold his stare when the tips of his fingers press close to my aching sex.

Angel hums deep in his throat. And fuck me, pretending it doesn't have an effect is taking all my concentration.

Someone calls out our order number and Angel grunts and lets go of my chin, satisfied he had the last word, I guess.

I close my eyes and suck in a breath. The spicy notes of his aftershave fill my nostrils, and I swear my pussy clenches at memories of his scent on my skin.

I don't know why he's doing this or saying things like that to me, but I need to come up with some sort of plan to protect myself.

If I don't, Angel Fury is likely to rip my heart

right out of my chest. And this time, I am not so sure I'll survive.

"Eat up. You're gonna need your strength," Angel says, interrupting my reverie as he drops a tray laden with heavenly scented food in front of me.

He sits down, taking a smoked chicken wing in his big tatted up hands and sticks the entire thing in his mouth, pulling out the bone clean.

Angel moans.

Fuck. Me.

CHAPTER FOUR-ANGEL

It's about twenty hours back home and we have a long way to go. But the roads are pretty clear, and I am enjoying the company so far.

Of course, if I really wanted to, I could drive us back to the Garden State tonight.

But why do that when I can hold Little Doll in my arms instead?

I'm pondering that very thing when I make the executive decision to pull over at a Marriot dotting the highway just after midnight. Koukla is snoring softly, and I grin at how fucking cute she is.

I use my phone to book us a room, a single, and I grab her suitcase and my duffle from the car, holding both in one hand as I lift her into my arms.

Seems like a lot, but I'm a big guy. She's tiny compared to me and holding her is easy.

Plus, I fucking like how she feels in my arms.

Her body is made for mine, and it's all I can do to keep my dick in my pants. But the next time I fuck Giselle it's going to be because she makes the first move.

I know I did something to send her running, and I'm not sure what exactly. My little Koukla has this wrong idea in her head that I cheated on her with another woman.

I'm not saying I never had more than one woman at a time. Because that's not true.

But I never cheated.

I was never involved with anyone like that. Never had a woman I called mine before.

How could I cheat on someone if I was still single? The answer is simple. I couldn't. And I didn't.

But with Giselle, things are different.

I don't feel single. I feel like hers. But the stubborn ass woman won't take the hint. I need to convince her of the truth.

I'm hers and she is mine.

My cock is rock fucking hard by the time I walk us to our room and use my phone to unlock the door.

I drop the bags and move to the bed, laying her down on top of the blankets.

She hums and turns towards me, and I can't help myself, I drop a kiss on her soft lips.

"Mmm, Angel?" she murmurs, and I grin.

"Yeah, Koukla. It's me," I whisper, brushing her wild curls from her face and cupping her cheeks.

"We home?"

The question hits me right in the chest.

Are we home?

I wish I could say yes, and that's a first. I've never taken a woman home with me. But I want to now. With Giselle.

Only Giselle.

I kiss her again softly and manage to answer her.

My whispered *not yet* falls on deaf ears and I gently pull the blanket out from under her and cover her with it.

I hurriedly check the room, securing the locks and making sure all is well before crawling in next to her.

My dick is aching, but she deserves more than to have me wake her up for sex. Mind blowing sex, for sure. But Giselle needs to understand what she is to me.

Hell, I need to understand what she is to me.

But in order for any of us to do that, I have to act better than I've been. So I content myself with wrapping my arms around her hot little body and snuggling her close.

Imagine that? Angel fucking Fury cuddling the night away with a soft woman in his arms.

I want to laugh at the irony, but I don't. This feels too important for that.

She feels too important.

We're in Virginia, and the truth is it's taking twice as long to get home with all the stops I insist on making.

I don't know what's wrong with me. I never have to play games with women. Hell. They usually climb over each other to get into my bed.

But not her.

In fact, Giselle seems hell bent on staying away from me, and maybe that's why I want her so badly.

It's a mind fuck, for sure.

Maybe it's her playing hard to get that's got me so hot for her, but I doubt it. Two long ass months since I've seen her, touched her, and it feels so right.

I suck in a breath, opening my mouth against her bountiful curls, curling my body around hers. And it's perfect. For the first time in all those weeks since she left, I feel myself relax.

And I finally sleep.

CHAPTER FIVE-GISELLE

My eyelids flutter, but I am determined to eke out every second I can get of whatever magical slumber I somehow fell into last night.

Mmm. Feels good. Warm.

I sigh and stretch and that's when I feel it, *er*, him.

Uh oh.

My eyes open, and I freeze in place. Behind me, or should I say coiled around me like the serpent he is, is Angel.

The man is like a giant anaconda.

So is his dick, a naughty voice whispers inside my head, and I bite my lip.

He has one arm beneath me, and it's wrapped around my chest where he is holding onto my breast beneath my tank top.

My nipples are hard. Angel's callused hand and rough arm feel so good pressed against them.

The need to moan is growing.

His other arm is snaked over my hip, past my soft belly, and his hand is buried inside my shorts.

This fucker is cupping my pussy in his sleep.

Truly, he is holding onto it. His fingers are positioned like my pussy is a freaking bowling ball.

That big hand of his is right over my sex, fingers right inside my wet, hot folds.

Like my vagina is his own personal property.

Like he fucking owns it.

I want to be angry.

I want to shove him away.

But if I am being honest, he feels so good there.

And to my utter shame, I wish he did. I wish Angel owned my pussy.

If only he wanted me like that.

But he doesn't.

Angel isn't possessive about me like that.

He's a born flirt, a womanizer. And he's human, despite all evidence to the contrary.

I am talking about his size and stamina, of course.

He looks like a superhero, or rather a supervillain. Like if some mad scientist took Thor's body and Loki's dark good looks and combined them to make one super fly motherfucker.

But Angel is no hero. He's not even a villain, though I am sure he does bad shit.

He's just a man. And men who like pussy don't generally turn it down when it's offered.

That's my fault. My mistake for giving away the milk and expecting him to buy the cow. Or whatever that fucking horribly sexist saying is.

Angel is just so much. He's fucking gorgeous and his body is to die for.

Literally.

I have no doubt he could crush a human skull with those giant, frying pan sized hands of his.

Probably as easily as he can make me come with them.

His fingers slide deeper, like he's testing my wetness, and this time I do moan.

Why does this feel so good?

Because its him. That's why. And I am not strong enough to deny myself this bit of forbidden pleasure.

I spread my legs wider, allowing him better access. And like the serpent I know he is, the viper lying in wait for the right opportunity, he strikes.

Angel pounces with zero hesitation. His blunt-tipped fingers delve between my pussy lips, and this time I do moan. Loudly.

Fuck.

I mean, am I wrong to react to his touch? I don't really think so.

Besides, it is not like there is a choice. I can't help it. My response to him is automatic. Like my body is conditioned to submit to his.

He's so damn sexy. His touch seems designed to turn me into a panting puddle of *please do me now* goo, even though he is still asleep and likely doesn't quite know who he is touching.

Damn him.

I guess I was caught up in Anna and Maria's amazing love stories and I thought for a second maybe I would have one too. But I'm not made for that.

I know who and what I am.

Angel and me, we don't match.

I'm too short, too chubby, and I have a big mouth. I can imagine what kind of woman he usually dates, and I doubt it is someone with a *size sixteen on good days* ass.

To put it plainly, I am not everyone's cup of tea.

The admission kind of breaks my heart. But I don't give in to that.

So, what if he looks like a Greek demigod come to life especially with that giant tattoo, the one that is supposed to protect you against the evil eye, inked across his throat?

It's no reason for a girl to lose her mind or her free will. I'm human. I have needs. And if he wants to take care of them while we are on this nut job of a road trip, who am I to deny either of us?

Angel never made declarations or promises. And yeah, he hurt me, but that's on me. I allowed it.

I can't blame him for taking what I so freely offered. It's my fault for not asking what it meant at the time.

The sex between us was good.

It can still be good, my inner slut says, but I squeeze my eyes shut, and whimper at the feel of him teasing along my slit, stopping when he reaches my hard little clit.

Fuck. Yeah. He's good at this.

So good, I can't even bring myself to look at another man, much less play with one of my adult toys. It just isn't the same.

Yeah, I'm in a funk. I'll get over it. I swear.

But right now, with his big dick pressing against me, one hand on my tit, and the other gliding between my slick folds, well, I'm only human, too.

I feel the hard bar of his cock pressed against my ass and I bite my lip to stop from moaning even if I can't help but wiggle against it.

"Fuck, Koukla, you're so goddamn wet. Tell me what you want, and I'll give it to you," he rumbles against my ear, and I gasp as he pushes two thick digits into my sopping wet heat.

He doesn't stop working those fingers in and out of my channel, and I can't help it. I press back against his cock, wishing it was filling me instead of his hand.

But no. I can't do that with him. Not without risking my heart.

"Tell me, Koukla, or I'll stop," he growls, and nips my neck with his teeth.

He's pinching my nipple with his other hand, and he starts to pull away.

But I stop him.

Fuck, I'm so weak.

I grab onto the wrist of the hand between my legs and I hold him there.

"Tell me," Angel demands mercilessly.

His voice is so deep and gravelly he sounds like a demon. And I fucking love it.

Stuck between a rock and a hard place, literally, I

am aware I should be shoving him away. I should yell or scream at him.

But the truth is, I've missed this. His body. His energy. The way he makes me feel.

He already knows I am turned on. My arousal is soaking my shorts and dripping down his hand.

What have I got to lose?

"I w-want you to make me come. Please, Angel," I beg.

"That's my Good Girl," he growls.

Then he starts to move his hand.

And I see stars.

CHAPTER SIX-ANGEL

After a few solid hours of sleep, I wake up with Sisi in my arms and my hands inside her clothes.

Even deep in my slumber I want this woman.

She smells so good. Like cinnamon apple pie. My fucking favorite.

She's so warm and sweet. I slide my hand lower, past her soft curls, parting her slick lips, and I groan deep in my throat when I find what I've been searching for.

Goddamn.

Little Doll's cunt is so fucking soaked. And it's all for me. I know I shouldn't touch her when she isn't awake yet, but that doesn't stop me.

Giselle is trying to deny whatever this is between

us, but I won't let her. This is one where I plan on winning. And yeah, I'll fight dirty if I have to.

She moans and I swear my eyes go crossed. Her pussy is sucking my fingers in, begging me to go deeper, and I oblige.

She is so good. So fucking slick.

Hot.

Tight.

Wet.

Perfect.

And mine.

I'm so goddamn hard I can't help but rub my dick on her ass while I finger fuck her into her wakefulness.

I know the second her eyes open, and I hold myself still, waiting for her to acknowledge me and the effect I have on her.

Poor Little Doll.

Her cunt pulses around me, and I know she wants it. She's starved for it.

For me.

That last part is important. Fireworks seem to go off inside my body every time I am with this woman, and I'm fucking positive she feels the same.

I won't even entertain the idea anyone else has

touched her since she took off for Florida. If I do, I'll go crazy.

Instead of dwelling on those dark thoughts, I think about the soft woman in my arms.

"Fuck, Koukla, you're so goddamn wet. Tell me what you want, and I'll give it to you," I say, plunging my fingers into her pussy.

She arches her back, allowing me to slide in deeper and pressing that sweet ass of hers against my cock.

I am ready to blow.

"Tell me, Koukla, or I'll stop," I tell her, biting her on the neck.

I love that spot. And how she reacts whenever I nip and suck on the sweet skin there.

Her pussy clenches. I pluck her nipple with my other hand but force myself to loosen my hold. I need her to say those words before I go any farther.

I think she's going to let me go and I want to howl in defeat, but at the last moment she clutches my wrist and I fucking grin.

I got her now.

"Tell me."

Seconds stretch between us, and I swear if she moves that ass against me one more time I'm coming with or without her.

Thankfully, my Little Doll wants me just as much as I want her. I just have to get her to admit it outside of bed. But I'll work on that later.

"I w-want you to make me come. Please, Angel," she begs me.

"That's my Good Girl."

I growl as I press my dick against her ass, grinding into her as I fuck her on my fingers, whispering dirty things in her ear.

"You're so fucking hot for it, aren't you, Little Doll?" I ask as I feel her start to spasm.

The sounds of her slick folds meeting my thrusts echo in the room, along with our heavy breathing. But it's not enough. I need more.

I press her down so her back is flat on the mattress and I move over her, kneeling between her splayed legs.

Her tank top is flimsy and light. She'd been teasing me with it all damn day. So, when I grab it and pull down, the sound of the straps snapping is like a fucking battle cry.

Both her bountiful breasts bounce free, and fuck, I can't take my eyes off her. She's so damn hot. Her green eyes are lust-glazed and that mouth of hers drops open on a silent scream.

So sexy.

Beautiful.

Mine.

"Angel," she moans my name, her hands running up whatever part of me she can reach.

I have three fingers buried in her cunt, and with my other hand, I'm reaching into my boxers. I pull my dick out, and her eyes go wide.

"Fuck," I growl, squeezing my dick.

I know what I'm about to do is sick. Depraved. I sure as fuck never did it before. But I feel a compulsion to do it, and I'm not a man who leashes his inner beast very often.

Sure, I promised myself I wouldn't bury my dick inside her until she asks me to. So, I won't. Not that.

But if Little Doll gets to come, then so do I. And this is what I want. I'm not asking her, and I doubt she will mind right now, since she's already half gone chasing her orgasm.

I can apologize later if she wants. But if I'm not coming in her, I figure this is the next best thing.

"Goddamn," I grunt, stroking my dick in time with the fingers I'm filling her with.

"Angel!" she screams, back arching, lifting her tits in the air for me.

It's too much. It's not enough. My eyes widen. I

take her in. The feel of her pussy fluttering around my fingers. The sound of her long, keening moan. The way she looks, so fucking perfect, with her tank top torn, her shorts pulled down, my fingers inside her cunt, and my name spilling from her lips.

And that's when I join her.

I rear up, sliding my fingers out of her pussy and lifting them to my mouth. I suck on them, savoring her heady flavors.

My cock jumps in my grip. It pulses. And I come all over her.

I can't take my eyes off my Koukla as my dick spits cum all over her soft, tanned flesh.

I can't help it. I am coming like it's my first time, covering her in thick white ropes of my seed.

"Angel," she whimpers, and I grunt in reply.

She's a mess. We both are. But she's never looked better.

And I let the vision burn into my brain before I run my hands over her, smearing it onto her skin.

Giselle is trying to catch her breath, but she doesn't stop my caveman display. In fact, her celery green eyes seem to glow with something primal.

The air between us is charged with whatever lust-filled craze we just shared. And I grin at the fact this little slip of a woman's crazy might just match mine.

I'm sure gonna find out.

CHAPTER SEVEN-GISELLE

"You want a coffee or something, Koukla?" Angel asks, and I refuse to even look at him.

He sighs, shaking his head as he places an order in the drive through.

We already used the restrooms at the gas station a few minutes ago. He orders two medium iced cappuccinos, and I admit I am surprised.

I figured him for a black coffee kinda guy.

Fine.

I am acting like a brat. And I know it.

Truth is, I'm kind of salty after waking up in bed with Angel.

The feel of his long, thick dick, rock hard against my ass. The way he looked jerking himself off, covering me in his cum, as he finished me with his fingers inside my pussy has me in a sour mood.

No, he did nothing wrong. I did not say no. He even told me to tell him what I wanted, and yeah, it was exactly what he did.

I was a willing participant.

Fine. I'll admit it.

Angel did everything right. And that's what has me so mad.

Of course, the jerk is just sitting in his dumb car, grinning like the Cheshire Cat as he raps his thumbs against the steering wheel.

Why? I have no idea.

His balls couldn't have been as blue as my ovaries.

I mean, I have no misgivings. I'm sure Angel has been with a dozen women since I left for my parents' condo.

If he has, then they must not have satisfied him, my inner voice reasons, and I roll my eyes.

Angel didn't lie. He didn't even have to try. That's how pathetic I am. All he had to do was snap his fingers, and I caved.

No promises. No seduction. Just raw animal attraction. And I was his.

Fuck.

I shouldn't have let him do that. It just confuses me. And I hate feeling this way.

"I can hear your thoughts, Little Doll, but I don't know why you're so angry. You wanted it just as much as I did. Come on, talk to me," he cajoles.

He's not wrong. I did want it. Maybe that's why I feel like shit about the whole thing.

Clearing the air isn't easy for me. I know I have this rep of being confrontational. Like tossing beer in Angel's face when I thought he was Nico.

But the truth is, it's easier for me to stick up for my family or my friends than it is for me to stick up for myself.

"I know," I reply, and pause while he gets our drinks.

I take them from him and sit them down in their holders. Then, I busy myself opening our environmentally safe straws and pushing them through the plastic tops as he pulls out of the lot.

They're not cardboard, and I am glad. I hate those. Nothing ruins coffee faster than having to sip it through a paper straw.

Anyway, the action is so normal. Just something a million other couples do every day when driving together.

But it's nothing we ever shared.

Our relationship has always been hot, frantic, sexual encounters, and none of the tenderness or normalcy others seem to have achieved with little effort.

I want that. And even though I am embarrassed by my need, it's time I own it.

I know it's a bad idea to get involved with Angel again. I just have to tell him.

"We'll be home in a couple of hours. You can nap if you want to," he says, breaking my reverie.

He looks pensive, like he cares, and that does something inside me I know I need to ignore.

It's a dangerous path to tread, thinking this man has feelings for me. He doesn't. I know he doesn't.

"I'm not tired," I reply.

"Okay. You wanna talk?" he asks, surprising me.

"I do. I mean, I have to tell you," I start, but it's so damn hard. I huff a breath and turn my head away. I can't look at him and say this.

"Look Angel, about what happened before—"

"Giselle, you can tell me anything," he says, shocking me, and I turn back to look at him with my mouth open.

"Look, I know what happened earlier was just everyday shenanigans for you, but it was a mistake.

And it can't happen again," I blurt, narrowing my eyes.

Angel doesn't answer, but his eyebrows narrow.

My nerves are beating me to death, but maybe that's because I just fucked myself. I mean resisting Angel's attentions doesn't seem like something I am capable of, so laying it out is the only way I know to do this.

I stew in my seat. My best friend is married to his cousin and my new bestie is married to his closest friend. There is no way we won't be running into one another, and I need to get this out.

"You didn't enjoy this morning?" he asks.

"No—" I start, but he slides me a look and I have to correct myself. "I mean, yeah, I enjoyed it. You know I did," I admit, "Angel, that's not the point."

He shakes his head.

"Then what is the point? I make you feel good, and you sure as fuck make me feel good. So, why can't we do that again?"

He makes it seem so simple.

"Because!" I practically shout the word.

"Because why? I need words, Koukla. Tell me why we can't do that again," he demands, and it's like I can't refuse him even though I try.

I close my eyes, willing some strength into my

spine. It's like he won't stop, won't relent, until I reveal every secret aspect of myself.

Angel won't be satisfied unless I rip my guts open for him. And I don't want to do that.

But I don't think I have a choice.

"Because I don't want to get caught in that revolving door you have of women desperate to get into your bed."

"Koukla—"

"No, please, just don't. Look, we're both consenting adults and everything we did before we both agreed to. But I just, I can't do that anymore."

"Giselle, look at me," he commands. "I would never do anything to hurt you. I'd never force myself on you, and if I made you feel like that, fuck, I'll have to kick my own fucking ass—"

He looks equal parts horrified and angry. And I don't blame him. But I can't let him think like that.

"Oh God, no! Angel, stop. You didn't do anything wrong. This is all me. You're a good man, I know you are. I swear, you never did anything to make me feel bad or pressured or anything. Quite the opposite, in fact," I mumble, forcing myself to get on with it.

"Then what is it, Koukla? Why'd you run? I don't understand," he asks.

Shit.

I know he won't stop until he gets what he wants. But I'm not sure I can explain my feelings.

It's not like I walked in on him fucking some girl. I mean, I showed up at the club without warning. And well, he was there, sitting in his usual spot with some skinny blonde on his lap.

She had her arms around his neck, and he wasn't doing a thing to get her off him. So, I left. I ran. Not just from the Vipers' Den, but from the whole fucking state.

"You have plenty of women, you don't need me. And well, I deserve more from a man than to be some booty call."

"Sisi—"

"No, you don't have to say nothing. I am not asking you to make me some half-assed promise here. I'm aware all you have to offer someone like me is a few hours in your office," I tell him, and I can't keep the sadness from tainting my voice.

"It's just I'm not made for casual flings. Not anymore," I say.

My voice is trembling, but I force myself to finish.

"Anyway, that's why we can't do what we did this morning again. It's not you. It's me."

"Sisi, I don't buy for a second that you don't want me as much as I want you. My dick didn't get hard by itself. You're sexy, young, unattached. Why not take advantage?"

"Oh my God!"

I gasp. Is he serious?

"It's okay, Little Doll. Your body's reactions are natural," Angel continues to mansplain to me, and I swear I might hit him.

"Excuse me?"

"Your body responds to mine. That sweet pussy gets all needy and wet. Fuck, Koukla, I bet if I reach over, I'll be able to feel how hot you are for me. This morning, I wasn't taking advantage. But the evidence of your attraction to me was soaking through your thin shorts. Don't be ashamed. But know this. While we're together, I'm all yours. You can use me anytime you like, Little Doll."

This cocky fucking bastard.

"Angel, I don't believe you—"

"What? That I want you? Here, I'll show you," he says, grabbing my hand and pulling it over the middle console so it's now flat on top of his hardening cock.

"See? I want you, alright."

Asshole.

He rubs my palm along his impressive boner, and of course, my pussy reacts. I feel my panties grow damp and I squirm.

Fuck this.

I try to remove my hand, but his grip is relentless. He doesn't let me pull away, just smirks and his cock jumps beneath my grip.

"See? You don't have to worry about me satisfying you, Little Doll. I am more than up for it."

"Fuck you," I snap and this time I succeed in pulling away.

"Not yet, Koukla. But when I do decide to fuck you, you'll be begging me. I got everything you need right here."

"Arrogant much?" I mutter.

"It ain't arrogance if it's the truth, Little Doll."

"Oh yeah? Well, you and your pencil dick can go fuck yourself. I have my own *boyfriend* who can take care of my needs whenever I want!" I tell him angrily.

"The fuck did you say?"

It's like the air gets sucked out of the car and I glance at Angel. He looks and sounds pissed.

Like really pissed.

But so am I.

"What's the matter? Can't understand me? I'll say it slow then. I. Don't. Need. You."

He grunts and jerks the wheel. I slap my hands against the dashboard as he cuts off an eighteen wheeler and pulls over on the shoulder of I95.

"Not that part," he says, turning to pin me with his icy stare.

"What fucking boyfriend?" Angel demands.

The temperature in the car seems to have jumped ten degrees and I am panting. But I don't know if it's because of the heat or the fact he looks so goddamn sexy with the vein in his neck jumping and his chiseled jaw set in a tight line.

"What?"

I lick my lips.

"Gimme a name, Koukla."

"There's n-no name," I say, moving back against the door as he leans forward.

Angel is so close. And he smells so good. Like spicy cologne and man.

"Don't you fucking try to protect him from me. I told you once, you're mine. And if some fucker thinks he can have what's mine, then I need to set him straight. Now give me a name."

"Oh my God. Um, I wasn't talking about a man," I whisper, embarrassment making my cheeks burn.

"Is it a woman? Doesn't matter. I'll let her know she needs to go, too. Now who is it?"

Angel is holding my face with one hand, and the other is resting on the console. It should make me uncomfortable. But it just makes me hot for him.

The fucker.

"Oh my God," I say, and I grip his wrist. But he is immovable.

"Angel, it's not a man or a woman," I hiss. "It's BOB!"

"Who the fuck is Bob?" he barks, and I see his fury growing.

"Let go of me," I growl, but he doesn't move.

"Koukla, explain."

"BOB is my battery-operated-boyfriend. My fucking vibrator, you jerk!"

Finally, he lets me shove him away.

"Vibrator," he says with a slow smile and a deep chuckle.

"Oh, Koukla, we are gonna have so much fun."

He pulls back onto the highway like nothing just happened and I am over here breathing like I ran three miles.

I shoulda lied and said no, but that would have been just as pitiful as lying about how my body lights up the second he looks at me with intent.

My heart is pounding inside my chest. And Angel is tapping his fingers against the steering wheel, murmuring the words to some old L.L. Cool J song.

He's even in tune. The jerk.

Shit.

I can't believe I told him all that. But I feel, well, relieved.

Like now, he knows the real issue. That I'm not some plaything he can take out when he's bored and toss aside when he's not.

It's a shame because looking at Angel, I mean, goddamn, looking at him, I feel like he's someone I could easily lose my heart to. And that's why this needs to stop. It's why I need to move on. Call it a self-preservation instinct.

The car feels stifling, and I swear I can feel anger and some other emotion rolling off him in waves. Angel doesn't respond. And I'm not surprised.

Not really.

But my chest aches, and I'm wringing my hands in my lap. We have two more hours in this car together, and I have a feeling I'm going to spend the whole time twiddling my thumbs.

Holy shit.

I just told Angel Fury *no*. And the shit for brains

just ignored me. He managed to dig out some very personal information.

It's like we've been fighting this battle, and even when I should have the upper hand, I don't. I am positive I just lost that round.

And it sucks.

In fact, I've never felt so raw in my entire life.

Angel Fury isn't the type of man to give up on something he wants, and whether it's about pride or sex or just for kicks, he's decided he wants me.

The question is, when I give in—*because that part is inevitable, I don't have the wherewithal to withstand a force as formidable as Angel Fury, so yeah, it is when I give in, not if*—will I survive the aftermath?

I sure as hell hope so.

CHAPTER EIGHT-ANGEL

This girl.

I am so fucking mad right now.

I've been driving for the last two hours in dead silence. I just can't open my fucking mouth. I'm totally unable to speak after what she just revealed.

Is she serious?

Does she think I'm some kind of male whore? Like I just fuck women without caring.

Shit.

Of course she does, my inner voice scolds.

Because that is exactly what I've been doing my entire life. One after the other. I've gone through more women than I can remember their name.

Using bodies just like they use me. Just to get off,

to relieve the pressure of my life. I don't feel bad about it.

Those women knew the deal, and they fucked me for the same reason. Just because I was there.

But this is not the same.

She's different.

The way I feel about her is different.

How does she not know that?

She don't know that because of you, you fucking asshole, my inner voice reminds me.

Now, I'm mad all over again. Fury fills my veins. It boils my blood and makes it hard to fucking breathe.

And it's all directed at me.

Only me.

Somewhere along the line, me and Sisi here, we got our wires crossed. But I'll be damned if Little Doll is just gonna dismiss me without giving me a chance.

Fuck that.

She's already mentioned something about me cheating or being with other women twice now, and I have yet to get a real fucking answer from her about it.

But I will. I've got to. There is no other choice.

I've been watching my cousin Nico for the past

few months. Seeing the way he is with his Anna, and it's unbelievable.

Of the three of us, Nico is a fucking wild card. I never thought he'd find his person. But what do you know? He has found her, and she is just as crazy about him as he is about her.

Watching those two set a switch off inside of me. It's like all my life has been a series of meaningless one night stands. I want something else now. I'm ready.

But Sisi's words, well, they cut me. They made me feel hollow. And I don't fucking like that.

I don't like her talking like she's resigned to some false belief that I used her to scratch some bodily itch.

If only it was that simple.

But the fact is, this ain't an itch. This is something more. Something life altering.

And I didn't use her. She's wrong about that. Yeah, she left town without a word, but that's on me, too.

It's my fault for not making sure she knows where she stands with me.

Shit.

The truth is, I'm fucking bad at this. Opening up.

Talking about my feelings. Fucking I can do, but she's right. She deserves more from me.

And she's gonna get it. I just don't know where to start.

I'm the Vipers' fucking Enforcer, not their poet. I never had to use pretty words or bring a girl gifts or flowers.

Fuck. I never had to.

Even Luc managed to get his girl. Maria, that pretty little bartender married him with hardly a fucking proposal.

"It's not you. It's me."

That's the last thing she said to me. I've been driving, my eyes on the road, just replaying her words over and over again like some kind of masochistic litany.

"Oh my God," she murmurs as we approach the street where she rents an apartment, and my eyes flick up.

"What the fuck?"

"Um, I think the building is condemned," I say as I come to a stop right along some police cars.

"B-but my things," she stutters, eyes wide.

"Excuse me, officer?" I ask, rolling down my window.

"Keep moving, buddy—oh shit. You're Angel Fury," the young cop murmurs.

"Nice to meet you, Officer Polaski," I say, reading his badge and offering my hand.

He takes it, and I raise my eyebrows as he simply holds onto me like we're fucking dating.

"Sorry, um, sir," he says.

"No worries. Tell me what's going on here."

He looks around, scratching the back of his neck. But no one is looking at us, and I know he's going to tell me what I want, and fast, too.

Most people do, and I'm right. It doesn't take long.

It's a fucking gift.

Whatever.

He explains there was something wrong with the gas lines in the old building and a few people had to be rushed to the hospital. That's not all. Apparently, while they were trying to fix the leak, there was a minor explosion and a subsequent fire.

"Which apartment took the brunt of the fire?" Sisi asks, and she is leaning over me.

The feel of her soft body against mine is playing havoc with my senses, but I don't move or acknowledge it. We have shit to discuss before any of that.

"Oh, the basement apartment," the officer replies, and I feel Sisi's shocked gasp before I hear it.

"Thanks," I say, and I continue to drive slowly down the block.

"That's my apartment," she whispers, and I know she is in shock or something.

"Oh my God. My clothes. My computer!"

"Your computer? Your laptop is in your suitcase," I say.

"Yeah, but I had a desktop for work."

I nod. I know she runs her own marketing business. I researched her months ago.

"Surely, you back up to a cloud. Can't you access it from your laptop?" I ask.

"Oh, um, yeah," she says and sounds surprised that I know anything about the stuff.

I'm not Steve Jobs or anything, but I know my way around computers and software. I have to know it. It's part of my job as Enforcer.

My legitimate title is head of security for Viper Enterprises, and it's the same fucking thing. The only difference is I only carry one weapon when I'm wearing that hat.

"But my laptop is older, so it's slow."

I make a sound, showing her I heard her.

It's no big deal replacing her computer, but I'm sure she must be feeling shitty about it.

"Um, I guess I need to find a place to stay."

"I got it covered," I tell her.

"Oh, no, I can't stay with you," she begins, shaking her head.

My anger returns with a vengeance. I pull over sharply, shifting into park. Then I turn as much as a guy my size can in this stupid fucking seat so I can see her face.

"Little Doll, look at me," I say, and I wait until her celery green stare meets mine.

"You said a lot of shit before, Sisi, and I listened, so now it's my turn. No interruptions," I tell her when she opens her mouth.

The air is vibrating with energy, and I know most of it is coming from me. But it's not all me, and that's the only thing I need to convince myself I'm right. That this thing between us is real.

"There's obviously been a miscommunication somewhere, but the first thing I want you to know is I was planning to drive you to your parents' house right now. Not because I don't want you to stay with me, I do. Very much. But I think you need time, and I'm sure this is shocking. By the way, I am sorry about your place. Of course, I had no idea this happened, or I wouldn't have driven here," I tell her and suddenly my chest feels tight.

I can't breathe. Fear is pounding through my blood, thundering inside my head like a runaway freight train.

What if we hadn't driven back from Florida?

What if she'd been inside when the explosion went off?

Our eyes meet and it's as if she just realized that same thing.

"Shit. Fuck. Come here," I say, and I grab her in a hug.

Giselle clings to me, and all the other shit I want to tell her leaves my brain.

She's hugging me so tight. My neck feels warm and wet, then I feel her whole body shake and I know she's crying.

Goddamn it.

I'm not good at this. I don't know how to give someone comfort, but I try. All I can do is fucking try.

I feel helpless and inadequate to the task, and it's a first. But I hold her to me. I feel her misery, her fear, and I take it all in. I take her in.

If I thought I was obsessed with this woman before, it is nothing to how I feel right now.

No, we ain't done. She ain't getting rid of me.

"You're just saying that cause you feel bad for me. You don't have to. It's okay. I'll be okay," she says, her voice muffled because she is speaking into my shirt.

I didn't even realize I said any of that out loud. Oh well. She might as well know my plans.

"Damn right you're okay, Koukla. I won't let you be anything else, you hear me?" I grumble, and I mean it.

I mean it so damn much.

The thought of her being anything other than whole, safe, and sound is too much for me to bear, so I don't even go there.

"You're fine. You're safe," I repeat against her soft, sweet smelling hair, "and you were right. You deserve a better man than the one I've been. But that's on me. But I need you to understand something. I'm not going anywhere, and neither are you. Not anymore. Not again. Got it?"

"What are you talking about?"

Giselle's muffled voice reaches me, and I smile. I love the feel of her in my embrace as she sniffles against my chest.

"Exactly what I said. I know you have doubts, but I have every intention of blowing those right out of the water. I'm the man you need, the one you deserve, me and no one else. And I'm gonna prove it to you."

I back up, and her arms slip away from me. Her nose is red, and her eyes are glassy. She looks sad and exhausted, but I don't know if that is physical or emotional.

Her eyes are still glassy, and her nose is pink from crying, and my heart feels like it might break from the way she is looking at me. Like she's scared to believe in me.

Goddamn.

I never wanted anyone to believe in me as much as I did her right then. But I am self-aware enough to know I need to earn that from her.

And I will. There is no other choice.

She is so beautiful. I can't help myself. I dip my head and steal a kiss, loving the way she responds even when she doesn't want to.

My Koukla leans her head back and opens her lips and I slide my tongue into her mouth twice before relenting.

Going home alone with a hard on isn't ideal, but I get it. She needs time and space. And I'm gonna give her everything she needs.

Me. Only me.

"Now, get back in your seat, Little Doll, and buckle up. I'm taking you to your parents' house."

CHAPTER NINE-GISELLE

This is not how I imagined I would end up at my age. Sleeping on my mother's couch.

FML.

After hours of tossing and turning, I finally pass out only to be woken up by a godawful racket.

"What the shit?"

Ugh. This is what's wrong with health conscious people.

I grunt and get up from the sofa at the sound of the blender going nuts.

Grabbing my phone, I check the time.

It's only five in the morning, and someone is about to get punched in the nose.

Angel dropped me off last night with a chaste

kiss on the lips and nothing more, and I have to admit I felt more than a little confused.

The things he said about his intentions and stuff really threw me for a loop. I have no idea if I believe him.

But I want to. And that's bad.

The second I allow myself to trust him, I know he's going to break my heart. I'm just not built to deal with all that.

Cheating.

Other woman drama.

Nope. Not me. But how can I expect a man like that to be satisfied with someone like me?

Ugh.

I hate that. Self-doubt is a nagging bitch, and I wish I didn't feel this way. But I'm no simpering virgin. I've had boyfriends and I've been cheated on. It sucks. And for some reason, I always take the blame.

It's always *you never try to hold my attention, Sisi* or *she's got the perfect body, I couldn't help it, Sisi*.

As if their dicks ruled their brains and their commitments to me meant nothing. Who knows? Maybe they didn't. Maybe I was the one in the wrong to expect a man to be faithful.

My own father strayed from the marriage bed and how my mother forgave him, I have no idea. But they're still together after thirty-seven years, and I know how hard they work at it.

Counseling helped. But I remember my mother's sadness and I remember promising myself I would never go through that.

So where does that leave me?

Alone. Or rather, on my parents' couch listening to my idiot sister make a protein shake at this ungodly hour.

"Resa, knock it off!" I shout.

"Oh shit, Sisi, is that you? Why are you on the couch?"

My sister is supposed to be dorming at her university, but she isn't getting along with her resident advisor. So, she's been commuting from home.

"Yeah, it's me. And I'm on the couch cause Mommy turned my old room into her crafting room," I grumble and walk into the kitchen in my underwear and long t-shirt.

"Shit, I forgot," she says

Resa isn't alone. Her boyfriend Dan is with her, and they are both dressed for whatever horrible exercise they're going to do.

"Morning," Dan says with a grin.

"It's definitely morning," I grumble, making sure my shirt is long enough to cover my fluffy ass.

"Sorry about the noise, Sisi. We have yoga then classes start at 8," she tells me.

I nod and start making a pot of coffee.

"It's fine. You need any help dealing with the RA?"

"Nah," she tells me. "I think it just has to work itself out," she says, and I note with amusement her curly hair is sticking up all over the place in her messy bun.

We have the same hair. But while I'm short and chunky, Resa is tall and willowy with a big butt most women envy.

She's beautiful, and I love her. But I know I can't live here long, or I just might murder her. And that would really piss our mother off.

"So, what are you going to do about your apartment?" Dan asks.

"I don't know. I have to try to figure out if anything is salvageable, I guess. Then I have to contact my clients, let them know what happened and that I'll be out of touch for a couple of days," I say, making a mental list of all the things that need doing.

We chat a little bit longer, then they both leave,

and I am all alone. But before I can fall into the abyss of self-pity I've been circling, my phone chimes.

I look down and I grin. It's a text from Anna.

> ANNA
> You're back? And you didn't call me!
> Sisi, pick up the damn phone!

I smile at her irritation. Anna has gotten super bossy since she's been married to Nico Fury. It suits her.

My bestie needed a little backbone, and that man seems to have provided her with more than enough.

I wait and pour myself a mug of steaming ambition, but before I can dial her number, I see her name flashing on the screen. It's a video call and I grimace, but I accept it.

"Giselle Vega, you have some serious explaining to do!"

"Oh my God, did you just *I Love Lucy* me?" I ask, and she holds her angry stare one more second before we both start giggling.

"Angel called Nico last night. He told him about the explosion. Now, don't freak out when you leave, but you have a security detail now just in case," she says, and I'm shaking my head.

"Security detail? In case of what?"

"Well, you're like my sister, Sisi. And well, Nico and the guys have enemies. If anyone knows our connection, they might come after you as collateral damage," she whispers, and I can hear the apology in her tone.

"Anyway, I wanted you to know you can use the condo for however long you need. Now that we moved. I mean, I know it's being renovated, but at least you will have your own space," she offers, and I have to admit my parents' place is packed.

Their apartment was always small. But with my room gone and Resa staying with her boyfriend while our parents are in Florida, I do feel cramped.

"I will definitely consider that, Anna. Thanks," I say. "But as for the security, I think that's jumping the gun. I don't need—"

But before I can finish there is a knock at the door.

"Hang on," I tell her just as I hear the sound of a baby crying.

"Oh, I'll call you back. Junior wants his breakfast," she says and hangs up before I can reply.

We've been talking for weeks since I've been away, but I know it's not the same as being in person. I missed so much of my best friend's new life and role as a mom.

How many of Nico Jr.'s milestones did I hear about after the fact? I've never even seen Anna's new home.

I suck.

I feel so guilty that my eyes tear up. They're just spilling down my cheeks when I pull the door open.

"Morning—what the fuck happened? Is someone here?" Angel says, pushing his way inside.

He thrusts a bag at me and takes a pistol from the back of his pants, looking around like some real live action movie hero with his gun in his hands. He checks the room with military precision, and I am too stunned to say anything.

"Little Doll?" he questions, coming back towards me and tucking the gun away.

"What? Oh! Nothing. No one is here. I was just—"

I shake my head, feeling a little silly. But he doesn't seem to care. He just steps right into my space and cradles my cheeks with his big hands.

Hands that were just holding a deadly weapon.

"You okay?" he whispers and his thumb pulls on my lower lip.

Icy blue eyes stare into mine, and I sway on my feet. It's like I'm being pulled towards him by some invisible force. Even more amazing, I think Angel might feel it, too.

"Koukla," he whispers, bending his head.

Then he kisses me, and it is the best I've felt all morning. Instead of pushing him away like I know I should, I lean into it. Into him.

Holy Christ.

He feels so good. Strong and warm. Like the September sun kissed his skin.

I can smell his soap clinging to his skin, and I imagine he's already had his workout. A man like him doesn't stay in such excellent shape without a vigorous health program.

But unlike most guys who work out, he doesn't preen. He doesn't have to.

Angel is a professional, and his muscles aren't for show. As if I needed a reminder after the way he came inside, gun in hand, eyes promising destruction to whoever or whatever he might have found. Which makes me wonder.

I slow the kiss, and he lets me, dropping his forehead to mine. Angel's breaths are warm against my face, and I love the way it feels. Like soft caresses against my skin.

He smells so good. Feels so good. I want to climb him like a tree.

I can't help it. He's everything I never knew I wanted in a man. I mean, he's enormous. So tall and wide, like he could be a professional athlete or something.

He makes me feel small, And that is no easy feat, let me tell you. Anna and I are both bigger girls. Chubby is the word polite people use. Fat is a mean word I grew up hearing a lot.

Especially from my cousins. My cousin Mikey is such a little prick. Every Thanksgiving he used to tell me I should just put my plate right in my back pocket cause it was all going to go straight to my ass, anyway.

Shithead.

The truth is Angel doesn't make me feel anything but good about myself. The way he looks at me?

Hell.

No one has ever looked at me like that. Like I'm something he wants to devour.

And I feel it down to my toes.

"Um, what's this I hear about security?" I ask.

"Who told you that?"

"Anna," I say.

"After last night, I did some checking. The Vipers have enemies, you know this. Besides, it's just a precaution."

"But I'm not a Viper," I say, waiting for him to answer.

But he doesn't. Angel just looks at me instead, and I am keenly aware of the fact I am standing there in a threadbare t-shirt and panties.

"We got a long day today. Gonna take you to see Anna first on the king's orders," he starts.

"Oh, but I need to see about my place," I interrupt.

"Already done, Little Doll. Everything that could be saved is in the back of my SUV, which brings me to the second thing we're doing, and that's moving you into the king's condo."

"How do you know about that? Anna only just asked," I reply, and again he just stares at me. Like he's waiting for me to catch up.

So bossy.

"Okay, fine. I'll go, I mean I can't sleep on this sofa another night," I grumble, and my stomach echoes the sound.

My cheeks grow warm with embarrassment. But that's my problem. I mean, obviously I eat.

Oh well, I'm only human.

"You, uh, hungry, Koukla?" he asks and gestures to the bag I am still holding.

I blink, still trying to find my feet. I swear it is

like every time he touches me, I lose all sight of where I am. This man has me so mixed up.

I am trying to establish a boundary, but it's like Angel doesn't even know what one is.

Why should he?

I doubt he's heard *no* very often. And if I am honest, I don't really want to tell him *no*.

But I also don't want my heart broken.

So, no, it is, I remind myself.

The man is like a bull. Just running roughshod over whatever perimeter I try to set up. He makes a noise deep in his throat and I swear I feel it in my core.

Why the hell is that so sexy?

"Brought you some buttered rolls and sliced fruit from Delilah's," he adds, naming Anna's bakery.

My bestie still owns it, but she has nothing to do with the day-to-day operation anymore, and I think she is happier that way.

"Oh, thanks. Are you hungry?" I ask, and his eyes roam down my body, stopping where the bottom of my shirt barely reaches the tops of my thighs.

"Always," he growls and moves forward, invading my space.

I bite my lip to stop from moaning, retreating a

step in the process. I tuck my wild hair behind my ears.

"I'm gonna grab a quick shower. Help yourself to coffee," I say and run to the bathroom.

I hear him chuckle, and my cheeks burn.

Fucker thinks he can waltz in here with all his manly hotness and throw me off balance?

Well, two can play that game.

BOYS

CHAPTER TEN-ANGEL

For some reason, September always reminds me of fall even though it doesn't start till the end of the month.

Still, I'm over here wanting pumpkin spice and apple cider donuts, but Koukla is dressed like she's going to the fucking beach.

She's wearing this bright white halter top that stops about two inches of skin above the long, gauzy, patchwork skirt she's wearing in a myriad of patterns, all with white, gold, and burgundy in them.

She looks good. Really good.

The skirt is long and flowy, so it should be more than decent. But the tantalizing glimpses of leg that peek through the slits in both sides make it sexy instead of Sunday school.

With her tits propped up by the top and that skirt hanging low on her hips, revealing her sexy as fuck belly button, I don't know where to look first.

Giselle's fashion sense is something between wild child and sex siren, and it has me all but panting for her.

The women I typically date don't ever look that soft or comfortable in their skin. They don't look free. They look hard and put together. Like they put in work to cover up what they see as flaws.

All plastic and cosmetics. Fake.

But not her. My Koukla is real. She is authentic.

She just *is*. And that is more than enough for me.

She's perfect.

She has this thin chain around her waist, and there are tiny beads dangling from it. Every time she moves the light catches it and my pulse starts to race.

I want to see her in nothing but that.

Wanna feel the cool metal against her warm skin.

Taste it, too.

I grind my teeth as we walk past a group of assholes who don't know better than to stare at my girl like she's a juicy fucking cheeseburger, and it's lunchtime.

I growl at them, and they jump where they stand, each of them looking away just before I lose my shit.

We're at some mall she found on the way to Nico and Anna's house. I don't want to be here, but she does, so here we are.

Giselle is busy picking out a gift for Junior. I already told her the kid has everything, but she insists she can't go empty-handed.

So, yeah, here I am, in a fucking shopping mall in the suburbs at eleven AM. The place is crawling with people, which I think is odd for a weekday.

But it's not. She reminds me folks are still school shopping.

It's late because we stopped by her old apartment. Little Doll insisted on going there first, and sucker that I am, I oblige her.

For the first time in my life, I want to make someone else happy, and when I say yes, she smiles. She's happy. So, yeah, I do what she wants.

"Put it on here," I hand my platinum card to the cashier after she rings everything up.

"Oh, but I wanted to pay," Giselle starts, but I just stare at her, and she gives in.

I put my card back in my wallet and take the bag from the cashier, then I turn to Giselle.

"Okay, I just have to stop at one more store. You don't have to come with me."

I look at her like she's nuts.

"Of course, I am coming with you."

"But I, uh, need some personal things," she murmurs, and her cheeks go pink.

"That's fine. Let's go," I tell her and gesture for her to lead the way.

We stop at a lingerie store, and I should wait outside. Really, I should. I mean it's kind of pushy of me to just follow her inside while she's picking out panties and shit, but I already know *Victoria's Secret*.

Plus, I don't want her out of my sight. Besides, I see a few men inside the store, so it's not like I'll stand out. There are boyfriends and husbands carrying their girls' shit and I grin.

Once upon a time, I'd have called them suckers. Now I want to be them. I want my woman to claim me like theirs did. She just needs a little convincing, and I can do that.

I frown when a guy with a measuring tape around his neck approaches Giselle while she's looking at bras.

The fuck?

He steps up to Giselle, grinning like a stupid fuck as he checks out her big tits in her tight little top.

"Hi there, I bet you haven't been measured in a while," he says still not noticing me.

"Oh, I'm okay. I know my size," she tells him, and

goes back to looking through a drawer filled with bras.

I step back, giving this asshole the chance to do the right thing. But he don't stop.

"You know the wrong size bra can lead to all kinds of physical ailments. Back pain. Sore nipples. I can help with that if you step into this dressing room," he says, leering at her, and now I know I'm gonna fuck him up.

"Excuse me?" Giselle narrows her eyes, but I don't give her a chance to tell this prick off.

Yes, he has a lesson coming. But that's my job.

I grab this fucker's neck.

"Eep!" he squeaks, but he can't talk.

I have my thumb pressing over his vocal cords.

Her eyes go wide, and she bites her lip, looking around to see if anyone notices. They don't. I make sure I smile so it looks like me and assface are friends.

"Make sure you use this when you're ready to pay. Me and Jimmy here are gonna go have a chat."

"Oh, um, Angel you don't have to—"

I drop a quick kiss on her lips and wink.

"Don't worry about a thing, Koukla. And don't leave this store without me."

"Okay, Angel," she complies, and I fucking love it.

I tighten the hand I have wrapped around Jimmy's skinny neck.

"Um, sir, you can't do this. I am just doing my job," Jimmy whines and tries to explain as I walk him towards the back of the store.

I shove him inside the employee restroom, and I lock it, blocking the exit.

"You always so fucking creepy with women customers, Jimmy?"

"No! I swear it."

"I see, so it's just *my girl* you thought it would be alright to get creepy with. Is that it?"

"No! No! I am creepy with everyone, I swear."

I frown harder. And I growl.

"Oh God, Don't hurt me," Jimmy drops to his knees, and I can see a wet spot spreading across the front of his khaki slacks.

"Fucking gross," I growl, then I slap him across the face. "Get up, you slimy fucking weasel," I tell him, and he obeys, still sniveling.

"Now, what you're gonna do is you're gonna quit this job."

"But I need my job—"

"You need your life more, right?" I ask and he whimpers.

What a piece of shit.

"I don't like you, Jimmy. You're a lowlife, hitting on women who are way out of your league, making them uncomfortable, and hiding behind your job to do it."

"I'm sorry. I'm sorry!"

"Don't be sorry, Jimmy. Be fucking better. Now, I'm gonna let you walk out of here, but if I ever catch you making comments like that to another woman, you won't be able to walk anymore, understand?"

"I understand! I understand!"

"Good. Now get the fuck out of here. And don't come back to this mall again."

"Thank you. Thank you!"

I open the door and step through it, finding Giselle on the other side, looking worried. Her eyes widen as a pee-stained Jimmy comes running out after me, his face a little flushed from his crying and the place I smacked him, but he's no worse for wear.

"Excuse me, s-sorry," he mumbles and mutters as he races out of the store,

Giselle turns to me.

"What happened there?"

"Nothing. Jimmy needed some job counseling," I tell her, shrugging my shoulders.

"I see," she replies, and she looks like she's fighting a grin.

So fucking perfect.

"Are you ready?" I ask, moving closer, breathing her in.

She always smells so good.

"Yeah, um, thanks," she says, handing me back my credit card, and I take the shopping bag from her.

"You didn't have to do that. I have my own money," she says, probably for the tenth time.

"I know you do."

"Then why'd you pay for that?"

"Cause I wanted to," I answer, placing my hand on the small of her back as we walk to the parking garage.

The trip to Nico's house takes another fifteen minutes, and Giselle sits quietly. I wonder if I did something wrong, but I push that thought away.

Doubting myself won't help me get her, so I need to focus on what I know and what I can control. I want Giselle. I need this woman in my life. And I want her to know I'm serious.

Whatever she needs to get there, I am going to provide it.

"Wow! Is this it?" she says, her eyes going wide.

The house is big, and yeah, it's nice. The cul de sac is quiet and safe, and I should know, I mean, I did all the security myself.

"Yeah. Wait for me."

I open the door for her. Her eyes are still on the house as I take her hand and pull her until she is standing. Her soft body meets mine in a whisper of a touch that sends shivers down my spine.

Visions of her by my side, us returning from some trip to our house, our home, fill my head, and fuck, I have never wanted anything as badly as I want that.

That vision, That dream. Me and her, together.

"Come on, Koukla," I whisper, taking her hand and leading her to the door.

Inside, she's whisked away from me in a frenzy of womanly squeals, hugs, and tears.

"'Sup," Luc greets me with a nod.

Apparently, Maria had to be a part of this reunion of friends. They're set up in the living room, and Mrs. Pirillo, Nico's longtime housekeeper walks in with the man of the hour, Junior, in her arms.

"Oh my God, Anna! He is perfect!"

Giselle covers her mouth, big tears running down her face. All three women are crying, and Nico and Luc look just as alarmed as I do. But then Sisi turns her head, catching me staring, and she does something I don't expect.

She smiles. It's wide and bright and it's all for me.

Then she mouths *thank you* as she moves to take the baby.

Thank you.

It's a fucking first, and I feel it down to my toes. I mean, I'm not the one people say thank you to. Usually, when I'm around, it means someone is about to get hurt or worse.

But here she is. Thanking me. And I feel another chunk in the armor I have around my heart give way.

To her. Only to her. All to her.

I am what I am out of necessity. And after the guys are convinced there will be no more tears forthcoming, we retreat to Nico's office to discuss business.

"Well, what have you found out?" Nico asks.

"The explosion was deliberate," Luc answers, and I grit my teeth.

"We sure?" I ask.

He nods and anger rises inside me like the tide.

"Who?"

"That's not so certain. We have a lot of enemies to begin with, but closing the ports, and the aftermath of taking down the Sanchez cartel, well, it left a lot of people feeling salty," the Council explains.

"Give me a fucking target," I snarl.

"Easy," Nico says. "I know you want answers, but for right now we need everyone on high alert. Tell all your men. I want double the guards on our private homes, on our women at all times, and at the Den."

"Done," I reply, and I am already texting my top guys to see it done.

I'd sent two teams to train at Sigma International Security under Josef Aziz and I know they are the men for the job. I spend the next ten minutes creating alpha and beta teams and assigning them to Anna, Maria, and Giselle.

I need to explain this to her. To let her know what's happening.

It's not the only surprise I have for her today, and it's probably not the one that will freak her out the most.

Baby steps.

Nico is saying something about Margaret O'Doyle, and I am barely listening until he snaps his fingers at me.

"Yo, I need you to go up there and represent us at this party in a few weeks. Luc is tied up with some legislation we're trying to get passed for our new real estate project. We're teaming up with Volkov

Industries to develop some land over in Bayonne. He can't spare the time."

My glance flicks to Luc, and he dips his chin, confirming what Nico said. I knew it was true, but still.

"Why can't you go?" I ask.

Nico raises his eyebrows. I don't usually question the king. But he also knows I hate black tie events.

True, my cousin wouldn't ask me unless he needed me. But still. I have to at least try to get out of it.

"Anna doesn't want to travel away from the baby just yet and I am not bringing him there. We need to show people the O'Doyles are our allies. Now, you can bring your girl or don't, I don't give a fuck. I can tell you, it's gonna be quite the affair. Margaret has a taste for both men and women, and she is all about celebrating her uprising. So, plenty of willing women if you're looking for something new—"

He's trying to goad me. And it works.

"Fuck you," I snap at him.

"Uh oh. Things not good on that front?" Nico asks.

"Yeah, bro, I thought you were going to Florida to bring her back to get her out of your system. Business as usual, right?" Luc asks.

These two pricks are trying to provoke me into giving something away. I know they are. And I know why. But it doesn't make me any less pissed at them.

Douchebags.

I've always been a *keep it casual* kind of guy when it comes to the ladies. But casual doesn't work with her.

Fucking my Koukla didn't get her out of my system. In fact, it only worked her deeper into it. I'm a fucking addict, and right now, I'm jonesing for a fix.

"You want me to say it? Fine. My looking days have been over since the moment that woman tossed a pint of beer in my face."

"Well, then I guess congratulations are in order, cousin," he says, and the motherfucker grins.

I sigh and accept the drink Luc pours and hands to me. The three of us raise our glasses and we toss them back.

I feel amped up after we finish up talking and walk into the living room where the three women, and one cute baby, are all chatting.

Like I'm getting ready to step into the ring.

When Koukla turns her head, and those celery green eyes of hers sparkle up at me. They are full of emotion, and I feel it echo deep inside me.

Now, I understand why I feel like this.

Like a gladiator entering the circle.

This is life or death. It's the one fight I can't lose.

She might try to deny it, but there is no getting away from me. All those pitiful excuses are meaningless. They are nothing.

Giselle Vega is mine. Now it's time I let her know.

CHAPTER ELEVEN-GISELLE

A couple of hours of girl time is exactly what I needed to start feeling like my old self.

Angel's gone quiet though, and I'm not sure how to start up a conversation with him. I want to thank him for what he did.

For coming to Florida to get me. For bringing me back home to see my friends.

I mean, family is great. I love mine. But I feel sort of lost in all the noise that comes with them sometimes.

Sometimes it's nice to just be with people you choose. And I chose Anna a long time ago. Same way I chose Maria, if only recently.

Sure, their men are a little scary, But that's okay. They treat them well, and that is all I need to know.

He pulls up at the valet stand and I recognize the building where Anna first came to live with Nico. It's gorgeous, and I am thrilled they are letting me stay.

"If you pop the trunk, I can get my bag and the box—"

I sigh as Angel steps out of the car. He walks to my door first, cutting off the attendant who was already making strides towards it. Angel says something and the man blushes, moving to the back of the vehicle to unload it.

The door opens and I take Angel's hand warily. I'm not ready for the tiny bolts of electricity that go zipping down my arm and spine, and I gasp.

"You okay?" he asks, and I nod, a small, fake smile on my lips.

It's after four o'clock, but the September sun is relentless. Sometimes I think it feels warmer now than it did in June.

"Everything goes upstairs," Angel says to the attendant, then he places his hand on the small of my back and guides me to the door.

I'm not really paying attention as we ride in the elevator. His hand is no longer touching me. Angel is busy with work, texting someone on his phone. But I still feel the impression of his touch. Like he branded me somehow.

And I wonder how I might feel if he really did. Brand me, that is.

Would I be happy and content like Anna and Maria if this big, powerful man claimed me as his?

I'm scared of the truth, so I ignore the entire thing.

I am supposed to meet the girls at the Den tonight. A sort of impromptu welcome home party, and I am excited. Thank goodness I still have a few cute outfits to choose from in my suitcase, because unfortunately, everything else I owned went up in smoke.

The elevator doors open, and I walk into the hallway. I startle as an enormous bald man with hulking muscles stands outside the door.

"Boss," he nods his head at Angel and moves out of the way, going to stand behind the security desk.

Angel dips his chin and moves to the biometric pad, placing his hand on it. I've seen Anna do it once or twice, and I'm curious as to why Angel has access.

"Go inside, Koukla," he says, nudging me forward, and I move ahead of him.

"Wow, they really changed everything," I

murmur, and take in all the new furniture and the paint on the walls.

My eyes immediately go to an enormous glass box sitting on a dark wood shelf that seems to be made for it. There are several glass boxes on the shelf.

Wait.

It's like a fish tank, but there's no water. My brain searches for the word.

Terrarium.

That's it. When there is no water inside, it is a terrarium.

I look closer and my heart pounds. Inside the largest one, I see something moving. It is dark and coiled, but when it slithers, light reflects off the scales, making its skin glitter like a thousand black diamonds.

"Oh my God," I murmur.

"That's Buffy. She can't hurt you," Angel says from behind me.

I eye the slithering serpent, and I think maybe he's lost his mind. She looks pretty fucking lethal to me.

Wait. Did he just say?

"Buffy? Like the Vampire Slayer?" I ask, and I can't hide my grin.

"Heck yeah," he replies, and I watch in shock as his cheeks go a dusky shade of pink as he walks up to the tank and eyes the little beastie.

"She's a badass lady. I had to give her a badass name."

I nod in approval.

He isn't wrong.

Buffy is a badass name.

I guess it makes sense for Nico to have a pet snake, or several. He is the king of the Vipers, after all. And I imagine it's not living with them because Anna doesn't want a snake around the baby.

Makes sense.

I have to admit the idea of that reptile is as exciting to me as it is frightening. Buffy lifts her head, and I watch with my eyes wide as her fork tongue snakes out of her mouth.

"She's scenting the air. Senses something new and sweet," Angel murmurs, and his voice is so deep it goes right through me.

I move closer to the tank. Buffy is covered in glittering black scales. Her head is small and really, she doesn't look all that tough.

But I know a little bit about snakes. They don't have to be scary to be deadly.

"You wanna touch her?" Angel asks from right behind me.

"Who me? No, I'm not brave enough."

I bite my lip, completely mesmerized by the movement within the glass tank. Buffy is thin, but she must be about six feet long. The tank is clean. I notice a large flat rock and a small branch inside.

"Now, that is something we'll have to agree to disagree. You're plenty brave, Koukla. And plenty smart not to want to get close to her. Buffy here is a black mamba, one of the deadliest snakes in the world."

"Oh my God! And you want me to touch her?" I ask, and glare at him.

"I asked you if you wanted to touch her. I never said I wanted you to," he corrects, and I roll my eyes at him.

"Same difference."

"Don't worry, Little Doll. I wouldn't let her hurt you. But if she did, rest assured in that little refrigerator beneath her habitat I have plenty of antivenin."

"Antivenin?"

"Sure. Do you know how mamba's attack? They're fast as lightning. First thing you feel is their fangs slicing through your skin. Next, your limbs start to tingle. And within minutes, your entire central nervous system is destroyed. A bite victim who doesn't get treated with antivenin suffers from painful seizures before they suffocate to death."

"That sounds horrible."

My eyes go wide. I wonder why anyone would want a creature like this in their midst.

"It is. And I've been bitten a few times. That's why the antivenin. I work with a local lab. I milk Buffy for her venom once a month, and they provide the antivenin."

Angel is looking at Buffy as she slowly moves about her tank. His icy pale eyes track her movements, and I'm tracking his.

I can't help it.

"Holy shit, Angel. Sounds dangerous," I whisper.

"It is if you don't know what you're doing. When you handle something like that, just remember, looks can be deceiving. Buffy might be small, but her venom is stronger than her bite."

"Oh," I murmur, and when I turn my head, he's right there.

I sway on my feet, and the responding rumble that comes from his chest tells me he notices.

Shit. I know I should know better. I should stay away from him.

But there is something about Angel that makes

me want to reach out and touch him whenever he's close.

Stop it. He's not yours.

"You, uh, want something to drink?"

Angel takes a step back, breaking the spell. I shake my head. But he's busy looking at where I have my hand pressed down over my heart. A subconscious attempt to control my runaway emotions, I guess.

I clear my throat and move to drop my hand, but he's faster than me. One big palm goes over mine, and I freeze. My chest rises and falls, and I squirm in place, trying so hard to not let him see how much I like his hands on me.

It's dumb. I mean, Angel knows I like his touches. How could he not?

He makes a humming sound and tucks a curl behind my ear. Then he turns away, leaving me with my thoughts and Buffy the badass snake.

I'm aware of him on the periphery of my vision. Angel takes his phone and keys out of his pocket. He puts them in a bowl by the door.

I frown.

It's so homey.

But I guess he would be at home here. Nico is his boss, *his king*, and his cousin.

I imagine being the Enforcer for the Vipers means he comes and goes often. Kind of like how he is with women. The thought makes my chest squeeze painfully and I close my eyes.

Don't go there, I tell myself, turning to peruse the rest of the condo.

There's a ladder and a toolbox along with a couple of crates holding what looks like tiles inside sitting in the hallway, and I wonder if the guest bathroom is also getting a remodel.

"Is the bedroom this way?" I ask, and yes, I am keenly aware the second I let the word come out of my mouth that I should have just stayed quiet.

Last thing I need to do is think about Angel and a bed in the same sentence.

"Hang on a second. Your stuff is here," he says and walks back to the door.

I watch as he places the box with the stuff from my apartment on the floor and takes my small suitcase from the guard.

"Okay. Let's get these to the bedroom," he murmurs, and gestures for me to move in front of him.

I walk down the hall slowly, aware that Angel is stalking behind me on silent feet. I don't know how he moves so quietly for such a big man, but he does.

Licking my lips as I try to settle my racing heartbeat, and I wonder in a moment of panic if he can hear it. I push the thought away.

Angel might look like a god. I mean, he has all the intensity and bad boy charm of Loki with the body of Thor, but he's only a man.

A fine as fuck man, but still a man.

Angel is not mine. I shouldn't be having any thoughts about him whatsoever.

Just keep telling yourself that, Sisi.

CHAPTER TWELVE-ANGEL

Goddamn.

She looks so fucking good.

I've got my Koukla inside the condo with me and I don't know what's harder, the pounding of my heart at having her in my personal space, or my dick at having her so close.

The way she moves is so careful. Like she doesn't want to take a wrong step, and it endears her to me.

She doesn't seem to know she can't do any wrong as far as I'm concerned, but I keep that bit to myself.

Just like I don't tell her this place is mine. Not yet, anyway.

After Nico bought Anna that house in the suburbs, I bought this condo from him. I've been doing the remodeling myself.

It's not that farfetched. Once upon a time, I worked construction. And I'm good with my hands.

But seeing her here I finally admit why I've been pushing so hard, doing all this work myself.

For her.

It's all for her.

I know I fucked up with this girl. I don't know how exactly, but whatever I did, I am sure it is my fault, and I own that.

The shit I've done in my life, it's, well, it's bad. I'm not a good person. But I can be good for her.

Giselle isn't like Anna or Maria. She has a family who loves her. A degree. She even has a small business she runs herself. And I'm so fucking proud of her.

But I am also aware of the fact she doesn't need me like her friends needed their men. Not like I need her, and it makes me edgy.

I want her to need me. But I don't want to change anything about her. She's been acting fidgety ever since waking up with my hand in her pants in that hotel room.

I know she wants to push me away, but I didn't chase her all the way to Florida to let her build walls between us.

No, I'm not happy about some douchebag

blowing up her apartment, but I'll take the opportunity to bring her here where I can keep her safe.

And do other things. Like maybe get her addicted to me. Maybe, if I can get her so hung up on my cock, just maybe this sexy little siren will agree to be mine.

I have every intention of protecting her, even if she says no.

But my plan is to win her back. To keep her. To own her.

It's sick. I know. But I won't apologize for it.

I need this woman.

My head hasn't been on right since she came storming into my life. But life with the Vipers means there is always something bigger at stake.

I have a lot of responsibility to Luc and Nico, and all the men and women who work for us. It's too much to risk being unfocused.

So, yeah, I mean to make Giselle Vega my woman. I have one goal, one intention, and that is to win her.

I'm no stranger to dark, underhanded methods, and I will do whatever it takes to secure my Little Doll to me.

Fuck yeah, I have a plan. One that is meticulously and carefully designed to woo her.

And that plan starts now.

CHAPTER THIRTEEN-GISELLE

I clear my throat to shake away all thoughts of how hot Angel really is, and I turn my attention to my surroundings.

It isn't easy. I mean, I feel his presence looming over me, and my body shivers with remembered passion.

Get a grip, Sisi, I scold myself.

Like the rest of the condo, the hallway has been recently painted. There are no fumes, but it is brighter than I remember, and there are no pictures or anything hanging up.

"Through here," he says, and I nod.

I remember where Anna was holed up for weeks with her pregnancy, but I pause as I enter the room.

The air isn't stale like it should be, considering

Anna and Nico moved out months ago. Like the rest of the place, it's been painted, and the furniture is different.

But even so, I expected it to be impersonal.

Like a hotel.

Maybe smelling of cleaning supplies or whatnot.

Maybe Anna called a service?

I mean, this is fast work. Even if Anna knew I was coming today, this is too quick for it to be for me.

The bedroom is also completely redone.

The enormous bed seems larger than a king and I take in the expensive-looking quilt and the dozen pillows on top. I can tell it was recently made. I take a deep breath, and every bone in my body freezes.

The scent of a familiar masculine cologne lingers in the air. My pulse starts to speed.

The whole room is done up on black and slate gray with silver accents, including the bedding. The wood floors are dark and freshly polished, and there is a plush throw rug at the foot of the bed.

The baby hairs on the back of my neck stand. Something is up.

It hits me and I feel like an idiot for not spotting it a mile away.

But I don't spot it. Not until Angel opens the

door to the enormous walk in closet, depositing my suitcase inside.

"Want me to unpack your things?" he asks nonchalantly.

"Oh my God! Are you staying here?" I practically shout.

Angel raises his perfect eyebrows and tilts his head like he's curious as to why I'm even asking.

"Considering it is my place, yeah, I'm staying here," he replies easily.

Thunder roars in my head, and I take a shaky step backwards.

It all makes sense.

How at home he is.

The changes in the condo.

Buffy the snake.

Fuck. Shit.

I can't do this. How the hell am I supposed to get over Angel if I am living with him?

And why didn't Anna tell me it was his place now?

"No," I say, shaking my head.

Panic and me, we're old friends, and I am about ten seconds from having a major attack. I have my phone in my hand, and I am already dialing Anna.

That heifer.

She had to know about this. I know she knows about this. She set me up!

That's the thing about people who are happy in their romantic lives. They think everyone else should be blissfully in love, too. And they meddle.

But Angel and me, we don't have that kind of relationship. We don't have any relationship, I remind myself.

Liar.

Shut up.

Frustration has me growling when it goes straight to voicemail.

"Easy, Little Doll," Angel says, and I feel his presence draw near.

"Coward," I mutter at my phone before turning to Angel.

"Thank you, but no thanks. I can't stay here," I tell him.

"You don't really have a choice. Wait a second, hang on," he says, moving to block my exit with his hands raised.

"Fuck you! I do so have a choice," I shout.

I'm so mad. I thought I was through with this man and his manipulations. I cross my arms, shaking my head when he moves to touch me.

"I don't know why you're doing this. Surely, you

can get other women in your bed, Angel. You don't need to try to trap me here—"

"Hey," he says, and my gaze flicks to his as I huff out a breath.

"First, I don't want anyone else in my bed. Second, I ain't trapping you, but the fact is, it's too dangerous for you to be anywhere else."

"What are you talking about?"

I exhale a deep breath and look at the ground. His pale blue eyes are so damn enticing, I know if I look at him, I'll melt.

Angel is the hottest man I know, and I have very little backbone when it comes to him.

Hence the reason I'm in this predicament.

Yeah, I wish things were different. I wish he was capable of having a real relationship with me.

But he's not.

I saw him with that skinny blonde. He has eclectic tastes in women, I guess. Or he just likes them all. Fuck, if I know. But I can't change what or who I am. And I shouldn't have to.

Simply put, I am through wanting things I can't have.

"Giselle, just wait a second. I didn't want to worry you before," he says.

"Whatever. It doesn't explain why Anna or Maria didn't tell me!"

Betrayal snakes up my spine, and I am about two seconds from letting angry tears wash down my face. I don't typically cry when I'm sad. It's usually a reaction to frustration or if I am seriously pissed.

Like I am now.

I try walking past him, but he takes me by my upper arms and slows my progress.

"Koukla, hold up. Anna and Maria didn't tell you because they knew how you'd react," he says.

He still uses that nickname he gave me the first time he saw me. It's Greek for something, but I haven't figured it out. Still, it does something to me whenever he says it.

It makes me wish I was his one and only. The only woman he uses nicknames for.

Stupid, Sisi. So stupid.

"To what? Being tricked into moving in with you because someone tried to blow up my apartment? No shit, I am mad. I mean, what the hell, Angel?"

"Goddamn it, woman, I'm not tricking you. And I'm telling you now," he growls.

"Better late than never, is that it?" I snap and I feel his anger grow.

It really is something to behold. Angel in a

temper, I mean. His eyes are glowing, and his chest is heaving as he tries to rein it in.

I'm not scared of him like this. I probably should be. I mean chubby or not, the man could snap me in two if he chose to.

But he won't. I trust him that much to know he would never hurt me physically. Emotionally is another story.

"And just to set the record straight, someone didn't *try* anything, Giselle, they fucking succeeded. Now look, you're associated with the Vipers through Anna. *Through me.*"

He sounds so fucking angry when he says that, and I don't know if it is at me or himself.

"Then can't you just assign me a bodyguard or something? I already told you I won't be your fuck buddy. I can't stay here," I say, shaking my head.

But he just narrows his eyes and pulls me tight against his body.

"No one guards this body but me," he states, and his voice sounds like he just swallowed a handful of gravel.

Holy hotness.

"Now look, I can't just let you go off and risk you getting hurt. So yeah, you're gonna stay right fucking here, Koukla. *With me.*"

"Angel I can't—"

"It ain't up for discussion. This is the only way I can keep you safe, understand? Now, I know we have a lot to talk about, but let's start by getting one thing clear. You are not my *fuck buddy*," he pauses and if it is for effect, then he's succeeded.

But what does he mean? Does he mean he doesn't want to fuck me?

That I am something else to him.

Something less.

His chest rumbles again and I swear it goes right to my needy little core. I squeeze my thighs together, and he inhales.

Oh my God. Can he smell my need?

I shake off that insane thought. Blame it on too many paranormal romance books courtesy of my bestie. Anna and Maria both are quite the avid readers, and they got me addicted to all the smutty goodness.

But Angel is no romance hero, and this isn't a fucking story. It's my life. And it's important.

"Then what am I?" I find the courage to ask.

"I thought you knew," he murmurs.

I shake my head, and his impossibly pale eyes roam over me from head to toe like hands. I bite back my moan.

"What are you, Little Doll? You. Are. Mine."

Angel seems to punctuate each word with a pause. By the time he is finished speaking, he is growling the words, not just saying them.

His chest is heaving, and his hands are holding me so tight, they're likely to leave bruises. And it's turning me on so hard.

So fucking hot.

My panties are soaked and all I can think about is how good he made me feel in that hotel room yesterday morning.

"Goddamn it. Look at you," he says, and I'm stunned beyond words at this point.

"Standing there so defiantly. Your breasts jiggling with every breath you take, tempting me to sin."

I stiffen and he just grins at me. The bastard.

"Oh, I can see it on your face, Koukla. You want to slap me? Go ahead. Do it,"

This time, I am the one tempted. But I don't. His words have me circling the edge, and it's too much to even imagine touching him at this point.

"You're trying to deny this, to deny us. But I know you want me like I want you. And I'm not a good enough man to deny us both a shot at pleasure," he says and bends down, claiming my mouth in a kiss that's punishing in its brutality.

I moan. I can't help it. Angel's kisses rip me open. They leave me bare and completely naked. The truth of my desire is right there in my response.

There is no hiding it anymore. It's like a living thing, and it can't be tamed or stopped.

It just keeps growing and growing until I'm no longer in control of my own actions.

I'm his. Utterly his. To do with as he pleases. And that scares the shit out of me.

"That's it, Koukla. Open that fucking mouth and show me what you like."

I can't deny him. So, I do. I open my mouth, and I slide my tongue inside his, tasting him just like he's tasting me.

I don't know what I'm doing. Okay, that's not true. I know damn well what I'm doing. But the truth is, Angel is right.

I don't want to fight it, either. Don't want to pretend or deny what's happening.

I just wanna feel.

"Are you wet for me, Little Doll? Have you soaked your panties?" he asks, walking me backwards until I feel the bed hit the backs of my thighs.

"Yes," I whisper, nodding my head.

"Good."

His big hands are sliding up my calves, to my

thighs, and I thank God I shaved this morning. My pussy clenches on air, my clit practically vibrating with need.

I'm so hot for him, I'm about to combust. His thick fingers coast over my panties and he moans.

"Fuck. You're soaked, Baby."

I nod. I am. Wet and horny. But Angel doesn't dip his fingers beneath the cotton like I expect him to. He kisses me again, and I give in to the demands of his searching lips.

I kiss him back with everything I have. I feel his hands move and I frown.

He's righting my clothes. Next, he's not even touching me anymore.

Wait. What?

I can't believe it. He's still pulling my skirt back into place. And I want to protest. I want to demand he do something about this state I am in.

A state that is all his fault.

But instead of taking me to bed and fucking me like I want him to, the big butthead just ends our kiss with a smacking sound of his lips against mine.

"Take a shower and get changed, Little Doll. I'll be back in a couple of hours."

"What? What are you doing? Where are you going?"

I gasp as he stands to his full height.

My head lolls back and I can't help but watch as he reaches inside his pants and adjusts his huge, hard dick.

I could help him with that. I want to.

"Angel—"

But he's already leaving the room, and I am sitting there completely stunned.

Angel turns back to me with a wink, his eyes grazing over my body. I'm exactly where he left me, my brain having a hard time processing what just happened, or rather, what didn't just happen.

"Two hours, Little Doll. Wear something nice. I'm taking you out to dinner when I get back."

CHAPTER FOURTEEN-ANGEL

I should have never told her to wear something pretty.

I can't stop staring at her and really, I should be concentrating on the road. But I can't. Not with the way she sits beside me, every movement sends a rustling sound through the car and fuck me, I'm jealous of her clothes.

That can't be normal. But still, I am. I want to be the one wrapped around her warm, soft flesh like the silky fabric she's wearing.

Goddamn, the woman is a siren. I breathe in her sweet scent and I want to groan.

Giselle is everywhere. Filling every corner of my brain.

And I like it.

I like it a lot.

She looks so goddamn good.

Sexy.

Hot.

Utterly fuckable.

If I thought she looked good before, Little Doll is setting records tonight.

She's all decked out in a skintight black skirt that ends just above her knees, and I wonder how the fuck she can even sit down in the thing.

Her blouse is cut obscenely low, sheer black with little diamond sparkles everywhere, so she glitters whenever she moves.

Her dark curls are floating around her shoulders, and they are thick and glossy. I am dying to get my hands on them.

I know exactly how soft it feels, and I'm covetous of it.

Fucking jealous of everyone else getting to see her hair all wild and hanging down her back like this.

Fuck.

Maybe I should have had one of the guys drive us. But I'm glad I didn't. Her cinnamon apple pie scent fills the car, and I groan, willing my dick to behave.

It doesn't.

I'm always fucking hard when I'm around her, and instead of being pissed about it, I decide to embrace it. This woman brings out the beast in me, and I learned a long time ago that it's better to feed that particular viper than to deny him.

"So, where are we going?" she asks, and I glance at her face.

Damn. She's so pretty.

Her eyes are translucent. Like crystals. And her lips are plump and glistening with whatever glossy stuff she used.

I wanna lick it off.

She is temptation itself. I want tonight to be special. I'm through beating around the bush.

This afternoon, I walked away from her when we were both primed and ready, and it damn near killed me.

But I only did that so she would understand I respect her. That she means more to me than sex.

I mean, I want sex. Of course, I want sex with her.

I'm only fucking human.

But this woman doesn't seem to understand the lengths I will go to ensure she is mine.

Body.

Heart.

And Soul.

I want to own her. To consume her. To nourish her. I want to be the only fucking thing she needs.

Sick? Maybe.

But I am what I fucking am.

So, yeah, I left her and me both unsatisfied to prove a point.

Giselle isn't some fuck. She's more than that.

And I am going to show her, starting with this dinner.

"You eat sushi, right?"

"It's my favorite," she replies with a smile, and I grin, too.

Of course, I know it's her favorite. But I'll take the sheer delight I see in her pretty green eyes as a victory.

I already asked Anna a million questions about her best friend over the past couple of months. Practically harassed the poor woman.

I'm not sure why she told me anything at all except for the fact I was so damn persistent. There was also the fact she threatened to have Nico cut my balls off if I hurt her friend.

Quite the little spitfire our queen is.

"Don't touch that door, Koukla," I tell Giselle when I see her go for the handle.

She knows better than that. But maybe she doesn't, and that's my fault. This woman deserves to be treated like a queen.

My queen.

I may have fucked it up before, but I'm better than that, and I mean to show her.

She sits there waiting for me and I realize I have yet to move. What can I say?

The woman turns my brains to utter mush.

My cock, though?

That she makes hard as fucking diamonds.

"We going inside or what?" Koukla teases.

"Oh, yeah, of course," I mutter and exit the driver's side and jog around to help her out, tossing my keys to the valet.

"This place is nice," she whispers, and I nod.

It is nice. And it is somewhere I should have taken her before.

As much as it pains me to admit, Giselle was not wrong when she said we never did things when I picked her up from Florida.

I mean we did *things*. But I never took her out.

There's no excuse. I mean, it's not like I was just

gonna come out and say I couldn't control myself around her.

She had me panting after her like a buck in rut. Or a viper on the prowl.

I have little experience wining and dining women. Usually, women trip over themselves, trying to entice me to their beds.

But anyone I ever fooled around with knew the deal. I don't do sleepovers, and I never come back for seconds. Hell, I never felt the need.

But with Giselle, all I feel is need.

Those other women? They meant nothing to me. Just like I meant nothing to them.

Nothing more than a temporary fix to satisfy a biological itch.

This isn't a temporary thing with Giselle. I know it's not. I don't just want her. I want to know her. Every thought swimming around inside that amazing brain of hers. I want her to share them with me freely. Hell, I think I might need her to.

Christ, I need her so fucking much.

My preoccupation with this woman is such it hasn't gone unnoticed. Nico and Luc haven't exactly been busting my balls lately. But it's only because they get it.

Hell, those two unhinged fuckers know exactly

what this kind of thing does to a man. My eyes flick over her and I swear I feel it in my soul.

Did I say preoccupation? What I feel is more than that. It is compulsive, possessive, obsessive. It is all those things and more.

I take a deep breath and open the passenger door. Giselle lifts her peridot gaze and my heart stutters. I take her small hand in mine.

She's so tiny and petite compared to me. I drag her out of the car, pressing my body against hers for one delicious moment before I make a humming sound of approval at the way she fits so good inside the cradle of my body.

Her curves are mouthwatering. Everything about her is enticing.

"You hungry?" I ask.

She bites her lip and nods. Excitement floods my system, and I can't wait to watch her eat. To be the one who provides for her.

My dick gets hard just thinking about it.

"Well, Big Guy? You gonna feed me or what?"

She is so fucking perfect.

Just like that, she gets me moving. I guide her into the restaurant and the whole time all I can think about is what I'm going to do to her after all this.

Yes, Koukla, I'm going to feed you. Don't worry your pretty little head about that.

CHAPTER FIFTEEN-GISELLE

"Here," Angel says, pouring me the last of the unfiltered saké.

It's sweet and delicious, and I accept the small glass.

"Thank you."

We managed to eat our way through an entire tower of sushi and sashimi delights. They seemed to know Angel here, and we didn't even have to order.

The head chef came out to greet us when we first got here, and they exchanged a few words in Japanese, which shocked the shit out of me. But I didn't ask any questions.

Truth is, I don't want him to brush me off. So I just sit and wait.

He's attentive, which isn't really new. But the setting is.

I bite my lip, thinking about how Angel held my hand the whole way to our table. He is the perfect gentleman, something I didn't expect from the big brutish man.

I kind of like this side of him. And I know I shouldn't. That I should keep my guard up. But it's so damn nice to go out with a good-looking man whose attention seems all for me.

This place is expensive and exclusive. There are beautiful people filling every table, and I've noticed more than one pair of eyes taking him in from head to toe.

I don't blame them. How often does a man like him walk through any door? He's enormous, handsome, and with those tattoos and the thick gages he has in his ears tonight, he looks like sin personified.

I know from Maria that Luc has some pretty kinky body piercings, and I wonder. I mean, yes, technically we've had sex. But it's always been rushed and half-clothed.

I've felt him. Touched him. But I've never seen Angel completely naked.

And I want to. I want him under bright lights so I can inspect every inch, memorize every detail.

Hell.

I think it's safe to say I have a very strong preoccupation with this man.

But I'm trying to break old habits here, and even though I am a bit miffed, he denied me an orgasm earlier, I am beginning to understand.

Maybe he's trying to woo me this time.

Hope sparks deep inside me, but I'm still afraid to grasp it.

"Your thoughts are loud, Koukla. Talk to me," he says, and his command is clear.

"What? Oh. Nothing. This is nice," I say, relenting under his brazen stare.

"Glad you like it."

He turns the conversation, and we talk about family.

"So it's just you and Resa?" he asks.

"Yeah. Mom and Dad wanted more children, but two girls were enough, or so my father always says," I joke.

I always feel like a bad sister and daughter for trying to have my own life. Starting my own business. Moving out when I was just out of school. But independence is important to me.

Funny how, with Angel, all I want is the opposite.

I don't want to be independent of him. I want

him to possess me. And I am not sure how to feel about that.

Does it make me weak or stupid or what?

I really don't know. But denial is getting tougher the longer we do this.

"What about you? Brothers or sisters?" I ask.

"Nah. Nico and Luc are my blood brothers, and Nico is my first cousin. But with Yiayia gone, that's it for family. Well, now I got a baby cousin, too, I guess," he says and grins at the mention of Nico and Anna's son.

"So, you're close to your sister?"

"Resa is like seven years younger, so not as much as maybe other siblings. But I mean, I would do anything for her," I tell him.

"Of course you would."

"What do you mean?" I ask.

"You're the most loyal, giving person I know. The way you stormed into the Den that first time, ready to take a piece out of me," he shakes his head and chuckles.

"In my defense I thought you were Nico," I say, and my cheeks are burning.

"And doesn't that make it worse? You were gonna take on the king for your best friend. I never saw anything like it. You are so brave. And you got such a big heart, Little Doll," he says, whispering the last bit and reaching out to touch my wrist.

Damn.

His words are like a balm to my soul and his fingers, well, they just feel so good wherever they touch me. I suck in a breath, and I just try to absorb them.

"Thank you. It's really nice to have someone say things like that to me."

"It's just the truth, Sisi."

Sharing little things about ourselves seems surreal. I mean, Angel is not the kind of man I expect to open up easily. But he does.

He tells me about his Greek grandmother who raised him. How she's the reason he is even alive today. And I wish she were here so I could thank her to.

"Is Koukla Greek?" I ask, suddenly stringing it together.

"It is," he tells me with a grin.

"What does it mean?" I ask, and he chuckles.

"Beautiful, Little Doll. It means you," he murmurs and lifts my hand by my wrist to drop a soft kiss on it.

Swoon.

I swear my ovaries are erupting like the fourth of July over here.

"Are you ready for dessert?"

He is asking a question that usually follows dinner. But my body has other ideas, and my blood starts heating.

"That kind of dessert you get later, Little Doll. Right now, I was thinking mochi," he replies with a knowing grin.

"Um, sure. I'll have the lavender green tea mochi, please," I tell the waitress, who unobtrusively appears at our table the second he says dessert.

She bows slightly and turns to Angel.

"I'll have the same."

After dinner, we drive to the Den, and I feel hyperaware of everything.

My brain keeps replaying what he said earlier, and I squeeze my thighs together.

That kind of dessert you get later.

Does he mean what I think he means? I hate to just assume he's talking about sex. I mean I know he wants me. But he's a virile kinda guy.

What if someone else in here catches his fancy? What then?

Shit. I am spiraling. And I refuse to do anything other than have a good time tonight.

Angel took me out for a fantastic dinner. He's giving me a place to stay. Protecting me against unseen enemies.

And I'm about to hang out with my girlfriends, which is something I haven't done in months.

I decide to shelf the innuendo he let slip earlier. I am an adult. If I want to have sex with a man, I can.

I just have to hang on to my heart.

Easy peasy, right?

But even as I try to coach myself, Angel opens my door, holding his tattooed hand out to me, and my heart stutters inside my chest.

"You ready, Little Doll?"

Casual sex Angel was difficult to turn down. But this Angel? The attentive, seemingly sincere one. Well, he might be damn near impossible to resist.

Am I ready? There's only one way to find out.

Gulp.

We enter from the back of the club, and I know it's the Vipers' private entrance.

Huge, hulking men who work under Angel line the hall and the entryways. Each door is opened for us, and I watch in awe as Angel's mien turns from one of heated attention to complete and utter no nonsense.

I understand. These men have to respect him. He

is the authority here, and he can't go around grinning and looking soft for them the way he does for me.

There is something completely and totally sexy about the way he handles himself. He is so fucking hot.

And dumb or not, I feel special being the woman on his arm.

Angel's presence is commanding. He moves with more grace than I imagined a man his size could.

Everything he does is with purpose.

He looks expensive.

Sexy.

Lethal.

He's dressed in all black and the result is, *well*, it's making me squirm. I feel lucky to be beside him. To be the one he chose.

His shirt and pants look like they are made of Italian linen.

They're soft. I know because throughout our meal Angel kept finding ways to touch me. He sat beside me, not across.

The better to share, he said, and I had zero complaints about the situation.

I imagine his clothes feel nice and light in the warm September air. My skirt is tight, but the material is stretchy, and the loose, low-cut top makes up for it.

My clothes are nowhere near as expensive as his clothes, and I think about how different our lives are.

Angel looks incredible, and right now, in my heels and provocative outfit I think maybe we match. I mean, I hope we do. But then my thoughts stray to that skinny blonde, and I stumble my next step.

"Easy," he murmurs, looking down at me with concern in his eyes as his hand grips my elbow.

Steadying me.

He's so strong. Like velvet covered steel. His movements are so smooth as he rights my misstep.

I have one second to get my head on straight before Angel is already leading me through the crowd, to the table where Anna and Maria are already seated with their guys.

"Gurrllll! You look hot!" Anna says and stands to grab me in a hug.

Nico is watching her like a hawk, and it doesn't escape my attention that Luc does the same when Maria tackle hugs me next.

Angel sits in an empty chair, his back to the wall, and the men all talk to each other in low voices.

After we finish hugging it out, Anna, Maria, and I join them.

We sit boy girl, and I feel butterflies in my stomach. They're both married and in love, and I am not sure what me and Angel are. But it's not that.

At least, I don't think so.

Don't you dare fall in love with him, I warn myself.

"Would you like a drink, Koukla?" Angel turns his attention to me, and I freeze.

His blue eyes are so pale and light, and all his focus on me, and fuck me, I wonder if maybe I'm not already halfway there.

"Little Doll?" he prompts, his thick eyebrows furrowing.

"Yeah. Sure. Um, surprise me." I nod as I squeeze my hands in my lap.

Angel nods his head, and one of the guards walks over. He gives them our order and I think he got me a lemon drop martini, which I am partial to, so I smile my thanks.

The music is loud, but it's good. The six of us are sitting, talking, and having a good time. At least, the women are. The men seem on alert, but I get it.

This is their place and since they are who they are, shit happens.

I notice there are more security guards, more of

Angel's men, on the floor than usual and I think it must have something to do with the enemies he mentioned earlier.

But they know how to do their jobs and to anyone else, they look like regular security and not a bunch of soldiers for the Vipers' crime syndicate.

I swallow.

Everything about Angel screams danger. But I can't help myself. Maybe I got a thing for bad boys. Or maybe it's just him.

Funny. I come from an average, middle class, warm, loving, and nosy as fuck family. It's easy to get lost in all the noise.

I am not familiar with violence. At least, not up close and personal. And it should bug me that Angel is a lawless, brutish man.

But it doesn't. He has never been violent towards me. In fact, quite the opposite.

My friends seem fine with their men, and their lifestyles. Maybe I'm just overthinking everything. And I am tired of doing that.

I want to feel good. To have fun. To enjoy the moment.

I'm thinking if moments are all Angel has to offer, maybe I should take them while I can. Squirrel them away for a rainy day.

Maybe Tennyson is right. I think back to my college lit class. Maybe it is better to have loved than to have never experienced love at all.

Oh my God. I am getting morose. That's it. No more thinking tonight.

I finish my drink, I feel loose and relaxed.

"Let's dance!" Maria shouts, and suddenly I'm being pulled to the dance floor.

I look at Angel and see him watching me, and I bite my lip.

"Yeah," I say, and I think I am ready for this. I hope I am.

"Let's dance."

CHAPTER SIXTEEN-ANGEL

I take every inch of the room in as I watch Giselle move away from me.

I hate it.

I want her next to me, by my fucking side.

But I can't just keep her there.

She's not a doll, even though I call her one.

My Koukla is a hundred percent real. She is a flesh and blood woman.

A woman who fucking owns me. But I don't think she knows it yet. And I won't tell her either.

I am not sure how to feel about this. About her seeming ownership of me.

I mean, it doesn't make it less real. There is absolutely nothing I wouldn't do for her. I just need to process it. To figure out what it really means before I run my mouth off.

I don't want to frighten her. She already ran from me once, and I can't let that happen again. She glances at me, looking worried, and I force myself to sit and smile.

It's not easy. All I want to do is growl and pace.

But Vipers don't growl. We're good at lying in wait in dark places. So I turn the heat down on my emotions and I exhale.

Maybe I should ask Nico and Luc what to do? How to get over this feeling I have, this need to possess her?

I turn my head and see those two crazy bastards staring just as hard at their women as I was at Giselle, and I think maybe I should keep my questions to myself.

Nico is steadily growling as his wife moves with her circle of friends, including my Koukla, to the center of the jam-packed dance floor.

I understand the way he feels.

My inner monster, that black as pitch fucking viper who feeds on vengeance and violence, is wound so fucking tightly it is all I can do to keep him silent.

But I swear to God, I'm liable to snap if one more motherfucker bumps into my woman as she moves in time with the rhythm and the bass of whatever fucking song that asshole DJ is playing.

I should tell him to play something else. Something with less bass.

Giselle is with Anna and Maria, and they are all shaking their asses and causing a commotion.

A group of pencil dicks dressed in whatever off the rack suits they went to work in this morning try to move on our women.

They're drinking and laughing, and I maybe recognize one of them as coming to the Den a few times before.

Well, not any fucking more.

One of them moves behind Maria. Like he's trying to get close to dance with her.

Luc growls, getting my attention. But it's Nico's echoing rattle that triggers my reaction as two other assholes try dancing with the girls. They are not reciprocating, of course, and that placates me. A little.

But I don't like how Giselle, Anna, and Maria are all trying to move away. One of them grabs her elbow, and I see red.

She shakes him off. But these guys don't take the fucking hint.

The three of us are already on our feet. And I am

mad. Nico and Luc are seething. I know how they feel.

I'm bigger and I muscle my way to the front of them.

Fury unfurls inside me like a cobra rising to his full height.

I grab two of these shitheads by their necks, and Nico and Luc have one each of the remaining offenders.

I raise my head, nodding at one of my guys. He knows what I want. He's fucking trained to know. A team of my guys is already in motion.

"Hey man, what the fuck?" one of these drunk chumps shout.

I give him a shake and drag him and his friends with me to the side door.

Luc and Nico are with me. The three of us toss them into the alley like the trash they are.

The women are safe. My men are watching them now. But this garbage needs to be taught a lesson.

"You fucking touched my wife," Luc rages.

"What? No! We didn't touch anyone's wife, man!"

"You know who we are?" Nico asks, and he sounds calm, which is a really bad fucking thing.

"Do you know who I am? I work for the mayor!"

I zero in on that guy. He was the one who tried to touch Giselle.

My Koukla.

"Look, we were just dancing with some sluts—"

That is all it takes. I am on that man faster than Nico or Luc can move. I hit him in the jaw, and he crashes to the floor.

But I pick him up.

He tried to touch what's mine.

And I hit him again.

He called her a slut.

I hear his nose crunch, and I know it's broken. But it's not enough.

This time a few teeth dribble out of his mouth along with a stream of crimson.

It's a deep, rich color.

I think of Giselle, and how pretty she looks in red.

She is so damn beautiful. And good. Too good for a guy like this to try to paw at her when she's just trying to let loose with friends.

One more hit and his jaw breaks.

"Stop! He's gonna kill him," one of the other guys screams.

But it sounds like he's getting punched now, too.

By Luc or Nico, I don't know.

All I know is anyone touching our women will get treated to this, or worse.

Because we are the motherfucking Vipers. And no one fucks with what's ours.

"He's done," I grunt, and drop him like the deadweight he is.

I don't know if he's alive. And I don't care.

I hear whimpering and sniffles. So, some of them are still alive. That's good.

They'll spread the word.

Luc and Nico are wiping their hands on the wet towels some of our guys brought out. The cleaning crew is here already.

I change my shirt for a solid black one that one of my guys is holding out to me.

I still feel amped, and he doesn't meet my gaze, which is good.

These pricks walk into our club and try to fuck with our women.

Hell no.

I am the Enforcer. No one gets away with this shit on my watch.

It's only been minutes, but I am anxious to get back.

Yes, I sent my guys to form a perimeter around

the three females who belong to us. But now I need to see her with my own eyes.

We walk back inside. The same dark energy coming off of me is rolling off Nico and Luc in waves.

People move out of our way.

Satisfaction rolls through me when I see two feet of space open up around them. My guys have discreetly pushed back the crowd, allowing our girls the ability to have some fun without being harassed.

I can't begin to count the number of times I witnessed a woman having to deal with some pushy asshole on the dance floor. As if every time a female wanted to let loose, it was some open invitation for fuckheads to come on to her.

It's something all women put up with. They shouldn't have to. It's fucked up. But that's life.

Well, for everyone else, maybe.

But not these women. Not *our* women.

Anna and Maria are oblivious, but Giselle notices. She looks around and sees my guys, sees the space they created just for them, and she turns to me.

Her celery green eyes sparkle like gems and my lungs seize. She is so fucking pretty.

She mouths *thank you* and pride fills me that I was able to do that for her. To create an atmosphere where she and her besties could just do whatever they wanted.

I nod my head slightly in acknowledgment, and she sends me a wink that goes straight to my aching cock. My eyes eat her up.

Her curves are fucking glorious, and when she moves her ass, bouncing around like that, I swear to God my cock jumps in time with her.

I want her.

I need her.

And it's time I told her what that means.

CHAPTER SEVENTEEN-ANGEL

ours later

All night long I've had my libido on a low simmer, but as we ride together in the elevator, it comes roaring back to a rolling boil.

"Angel," she says my name, but I shake my head.

She closes her mouth as the cabin opens. I nod my head at my guard, and I take her arm, leading her to the front door.

I can't let her speak. Definitely can't hear her say my name. If I listen to that husky voice of hers, I might come in my pants.

My heart is thundering inside my chest like hooves of the four horsemen of the apocalypse. Something is about to change.

My entire world. And it all hinges on whether

she says yes. I slam the door shut and turn her by her arm to face me. I'm not gentle. I can't be.

"Angel, I—"

"Shh. Don't say anything, Little Doll. Just answer one question for me," I interrupt her.

She nods, eyebrows raised expectantly.

"Will you let me fuck you tonight?"

It's crude.

It's lewd.

I know it, and judging from the way her eyes widen, she knows it, too.

She deserves better, but I can't be someone I'm not. And something tells me my Little Doll likes me the way I am.

Rough and raw.

Hot and needy.

For her.

Only for her.

All for her.

It's been months since I've been buried balls deep inside her dripping cunt. That little touchy feely shit in the hotel did nothing to take the edge off.

It only made me want her more.

I wait on tenterhooks, barely breathing until she finally opens her mouth to answer me.

"Yes, Angel. I'll let you fuck me tonight."

My eyes close, like I'm offering a prayer of thanks to whatever deity made this all possible. Next, I pounce.

The gloves are fucking off now, Koukla.

If I'm going to show her what I feel for her, maybe starting with my body isn't a bad thing. We've got a chemistry that is off the charts.

Most of the time, sex is perfunctory for me. But not with her. With Giselle, it's transcendent.

It's like her body was made for mine. I'm no slouch. I know she's got a thing for me, too. I can see it every time she looks at me. Like now.

It's not conceit, it's fact.

I'm fit.

I have to be.

My muscles aren't just for show. And the tattoos, well, those I got for various reasons.

Some people might think I look like a monster. I'm six and a half feet tall and every inch of me is covered in thick ropes of muscle and ink. Only my chest is bare, and that's because I reserved that one place over my heart for something special.

Something like this. Like her.

But I am not ready to admit that yet, so I just continue to shuck off my clothes. Her eyes go wide as I remove my buckle and undo my pants, kicking my shoes off.

"Clothes. Off. Now."

Fuck me.

She's got me reduced to one word sentences. But she doesn't seem to mind.

Giselle exhales sharply, but she's already unzipping her skirt, tugging the tight material over her hips and bending down to take it off.

"Leave the shoes," I growl, and she swallows.

Next, she takes off her blouse, and I almost fucking fall down.

She is standing there clad only in her matching bra and panties, both made out of some sheer nude material revealing every inch of her delicious body, and those goddamn fuck me heels.

Shit. Fuck.

I reach for her and pull her close. Even in heels, she is so much smaller than me. So petite and precious. And I fucking love it.

Little Doll is perfect. Her soft curves fit my hard body, and I love the feel of her weight in my hands as I grab her by the ass and lift her off the floor.

"Angel!" she startles.

But I'm not backing down. In fact, I am already swallowing the sound of her pitiful protests.

The caged beast that dwells deep inside me, the one I keep hidden from most of the world starts to wake.

It's like my darkness is attracted to the light in her, and when I have her in my arms like this, I can't spare the energy to keep that part of me locked away.

And it's okay. I don't have to. Even that unhinged fucking part of me won't hurt her. It's something I'm just not capable of.

Not ever.

I lick into her mouth. The taste of sugar and lemons dances across my tongue and I moan.

I squeeze her ass cheeks, pushing one hand further between her legs until I find her soaked and hot, those puny panties doing nothing to hide her from me.

"Damn, Little Doll. You're so goddam wet, so hot. This all for me? Tell me," I growl against her mouth.

"Please," she begs.

But I won't be moved. Not until she gives me what I want.

"Tell me who owns this fucking body."

I should be patient, calm, and gentle.

All those things.

But I'm not. It's just not part of my chemical

makeup. And I might want Koukla for everything she is, but I need her to want me for all that I am.

No more. No less.

I want her to take me as I am. To crave all of me the way I crave her.

All the good and bad bits. The sick, fucking depraved parts of my soul.

Blood is thundering through my veins, and I feel more animal than man. Giselle's eyes widen and her lips part as I coast my fingers across her clit.

I give her sex a wet sounding slap.

"Tell me."

Giselle's eyes are sparkling up at me, and her lips part. They're red and swollen from my rough kisses. And I can't wait to see them wrapped around my cock.

Not tonight.

But soon.

"You do. You own it, Angel, please," she whimpers, and I toss her onto the mattress.

I don't look away as she bounces. I just lick my lips and reach for the front snap on her bra, freeing her magnificent tits.

"Fucking perfect," I grunt and push her back, latching onto one nipple like my life depends on it.

Maybe it does. God knows, my fucking sanity depends on this little siren.

I'm crazy for her. Mad with desire.

Giselle arches against me and moans. But I don't spend long sucking her tits. I can't. I'm so amped, I'm ready to blow.

But I need more. I need to taste her all over.

This isn't something I've done with her. But it feels necessary. Like some urgent biological imperative is pushing me to lick my woman from head to toe, to stamp myself all over her.

With my spit.

My cum.

My sweat.

My promise.

"Drop your legs open," I command, tapping her knees.

Her curls are glistening even through her sheer panties. I grab the elastic at the top, tearing them off her body, ignoring her whimpered gasp.

"Delicious," I grunt before bending down.

I give her no time to get used to the idea. I just fall in.

I press my whole fucking face against her pussy, and I slide my tongue in deep. Her cunt contracts around me, and I feel it down to my balls.

Giselle yells. She slaps at my shoulders, grabs onto my head, but I don't stop.

I fuck her on my tongue, then I retreat, pushing three fingers inside her tight sheath as I lap at her tight little asshole.

I wanna fuck her there, too.

I plan on it. And I tell her.

"So fucking perfect, Koukla. Gonna fuck this ass after I fill your hot cunt with my cum. Want that, Little Doll?" I ask.

Giselle nods her head. She's so fucking turned on. I feel her pussy flutter as I tease her forbidden hole with my pinky and slide the rest of my fingers in and out of her tight cunt.

"Yeah. You want that," I tell her as I swap out my hand for the head of my cock.

"Angel, need you," she moans, flexing her hips as she tries to entice me forward.

"It's about fucking time," I growl, and I push in hard.

Her pussy stretches to accommodate my thick cock, and I know I should wait, but I can't. My hand wraps around her throat and I crush my lips to hers, forcing her mouth open.

My eyes are glued to hers as I fuck her, ramming my tongue in her throat in time with my dick.

It's brutal. It's not tender or soft. Not how I wanted to be with her.

But I can't fucking help it. The beast is unleashed.

My inner viper poised and primed as I pound into her hot, tight body.

Her tits press against my chest. They're so fucking soft. I want to bite them. To mark them as mine.

Our eyes are locked, and I can't help but feel that isn't the only thing. This woman has me. She might not know it or understand what it means, but she has me.

I lift my head. My hips are still thrusting, but I force myself to slow down. I adjust my angle, lengthening my movements so I am stroking her long and deep inside.

I get it right. I feel the second I rub along that secret place inside her. Giselle's eyes flutter and her pussy clenches around me. I grind my pubis against her clit. And she starts to come.

"That's it. Come for me. Good Girl. Squeeze me tight with those fucking thighs," I growl.

"Angel," she sighs my name.

Poor Little Doll is tired. But I ain't through.

I slide my dick out of her still pulsing cunt, and I turn her over.

"This fucking ass," I groan and spread her cheeks, licking her tight hole.

"Angel," she whimpers pitifully, and squirms to try to get away.

But I've already had my mouth on her here, and I want more. I'm relentless. I want all of her.

I reach into the side drawer and pull out a fresh bottle of lube, squeezing some into my hand.

I coat my fingers and tease it along her tight hole. My need is building. It is coursing, burning, growing with each passing second.

I know I won't be sated until I fuck every hole of hers. And I want in here next.

"Easy, Little Doll. That's it, relax," I instruct her, one hand is strumming her clit, the other is pushing inside her asshole.

Giselle is panting, and I know I am stretching her as I slide another finger in.

Her muscles expand and tighten around my fingers. The lube making it easier for me to slide in and out, but I need her ready and needy before I can stick my thick cock inside her.

I have one hand strumming her clit, playing her like a melody while I fuck her ass on my fingers. I stop my fiddling and lower my hand to feel the wetness dripping from her pussy.

My dirty Little Doll likes it when I do this.

She likes it a lot.

As if to prove my conclusions correct, Giselle moans and pushes back, sucking my fingers deeper inside her tight little asshole.

And now I'm even more turned on.

"Gonna fuck this virgin asshole, my Koukla. Gonna make it feel so good for you. Ready?" I ask, and I'm kneeling behind her.

I can't wait anymore, and three fingers in her ass is enough, I think. She is good and stretched. Ready for me, I hope. I pull them out, rubbing them up and down my dick, lubing my cock so I don't hurt her.

I will never do that.

Not ever.

"Fuck. You're so tight," I growl, notching my leaking tip inside of her.

Giselle moans and the sound is low and deep as I push my dick inside her tight asshole, past the first ring of muscles.

"Fuck."

I freeze, not sure how far to go. But Giselle, well, she takes the reins from my hands. It's like even though I know she's never done this, she wants it so badly, wants me so badly, she breathes through the discomfort and relaxes her sweet fucking body.

The victory of it roars inside my soul. And I want to echo it, but I can't lose control. I have to be sure to please my Little Doll. To make this as perfect for her as she's making it for me.

"Angel," she says my name, and it sounds like a prayer spilling from her lips.

She lowers her head and relaxes her body, pressing back, taking me deeper.

I won't lie. I've done this before. But with women who did this shit on the daily. Not with anyone like her.

I feel like a fucking virgin as I take her sweet ass. And she is the perfect woman to help me through it. Giselle isn't shy like I expect her to be. She takes what she needs, and I am so fucking proud of her.

Proud that she is so confident. So damn sexy. And so fucking proud to be the one she chooses.

"That's it, Koukla. Keep rocking that ass back into me. Take everything you need. Everything you want. I got it all for you," I tell her, praising her and running my hands over her shoulders, her back, her ass.

I find her clit again, and I squeeze the tight nubbin. Her moans and pants urge me on. Now, I am moving with her, filling her ass, my balls slapping against the backs of her thighs.

"Gonna come. Oh, God! I'm gonna come," she cries out, and I am so right there with her.

Her back arches just as my cock explodes, and I groan long and hard as I fill her with hot ropes of cum until it's dripping down my balls and both our thighs.

After some minutes, I pull out of her slowly and note her wince.

Shit.

Was I too rough? Fuck.

I frown and smooth my hands down her back soothingly.

"Are you okay?" I ask, dropping quick kisses on her soft skin.

"I am so okay," Giselle replies, and a deep exhale leaves her parted lips.

Her cheeks are all pink and she is breathless. She looks so damn good.

Deliciously dirty.

Well-fucked.

Happy.

My heart stops when she turns to look at me over her shoulder with a naughty grin on her face.

Mine. She looks like mine.

I feel so damn full of emotion, near to bursting.

The least of which is not possessive. Sisi is a free spirit, but she is my free spirit.

I'm obsessed. Devoted. Totally fixated on this woman.

Goddamn.

I need her to be mine. To accept the fact she ain't going anywhere.

She moans softly. The sound is one of contentment as she straightens her legs and lies face down on my bed.

Just that is enough for my dick to be ready to go another round. But I saw her wince earlier and before I fuck her again, I'm thinking we both need to clean up and rest a bit.

"Come here, Koukla," I whisper and stand beside the bed, lifting her up before she can protest.

Ten minutes later, we are both soaking in the enormous bathtub, and I have her seated on my lap.

And it's exactly where I want her.

CHAPTER EIGHTEEN-GISELLE

The morning after the big date, after Angel fucks my ass for the first time ever, I wake up feeling a million different things.

The least of which is not completely satisfied.

I never thought I would like to have sex *there*. And honestly, if any other man attempted it, I would have likely knocked him over the head.

But Angel is just so, well, perfect.

Other men never know what to do with me. Not that there have been many, but still.

Not Angel, though. He is so confident and certain. So sensual and earthy. He knows exactly how to handle my body. How to conjure pleasure so pure, it's sheer ecstasy.

A cramp starts low in my stomach, and I muffle

my groan.

Damn.

I know I am getting my period. Like any second now.

My stomach does another twist, and I rush to the bathroom. I always get nauseous on the first day of my menstrual cycle.

So now here I am, in a gorgeous penthouse condo owned by one of the sexiest men alive. A man who had his big, thick cock inside my ass not six hours ago, making me feel like a sex goddess, and causing me to come so hard I definitely passed out for a few seconds afterwards.

And I'm bent over his toilet, dry heaving like I'm hung over. If ever a black hole could just open up and swallow someone alive, I wish it would happen right now.

But it doesn't.

I heave again and feel the start of what are going to be some really shitty cramps coming on.

It takes a few more minutes of me just spitting out nothing in the toilet to settle my upset stomach. Just when I get it under control, I feel something cool pressing on the back of my neck.

I turn my head, and I see Angel. He's holding a

wet hand towel against the back of my neck, my hair is lifted in his other hand. He looks concerned.

"I'm not pregnant. It's my period," I blurt, and he frowns harder.

"I wasn't gonna go there first, Koukla. I was worried maybe the sushi didn't sit right," he replies.

His voice is deep, but it's soft. Almost tender, tentative even, like his touch, and it's so contrary to how he handled me last night. But right here, it seems appropriate, and I think maybe I fall for him a little bit more.

Fuck, I am so embarrassed.

And why didn't I think of bad sushi? It's not like men naturally assume a woman is pregnant just because she gets sick. But I think I must be panicking a little.

That's probably because the idea of having his baby doesn't scare me half as much as it should.

Don't even think about it, I tell myself.

But I can imagine myself holding a beautiful blue-eyed baby and I shiver.

I am so fucked.

It's a ridiculous thought to have. I mean, I literally left the state because the idea of this man cheating on me was too much to handle. Imagine how I would feel if I was pregnant, and he just left me for someone else?

It's too much to bear, so I don't think about it for long.

I feel so confused. Angel is looking at me expectantly, and I want to scream.

Ugh, why is he so sexy first thing in the morning?

I take in his short hair, almost buzzed to his skull, and the fact he is shirtless. The boxer briefs he has on outline his half-hard cock and goddamn, I am ready to drool. Then I get another cramp, and I wince.

"Hey, it's gonna be okay," Angel whispers.

I close my eyes and bite my lip.

"What can I do for you, Little Doll? Tell me what you need," he says, and I close my eyes.

Angel is usually a lot, but this is almost too much. I mean, does he really care about me, or is this just him?

Like, is this part of the whole experience of fucking Angel Fury?

It's petty, and I am not proud of those thoughts. But I don't stop having them. And I don't think I am mature enough to deal with my apparent jealousy.

He's so damn cute when he looks at me all confused and concerned.

So sexy.

He is really too good sometimes. But I think we should address the elephant in the room. The one I just brought up by blurting the fact I'm not pregnant.

"Oh, um, I think I have what I need in my suitcase," I finally answer him, and I slide my butt down, so I am sitting on the cool tile.

"But there is something I think we need to discuss, that is," I trail off.

"Whatever it is, you can tell me, Little Doll."

And just like that, I'm undone.

CHAPTER NINETEEN-GISELLE

"Okay," I say, and bite my lip as he joins me on the floor of the ridiculously large bathroom.

"It's just, I know we haven't talked about it, but maybe we should," I hedge and again I feel like a moron.

Safe sex is not something anyone should take for granted. I should have had this discussion before I ever touched him. And I am not proud I haven't.

"Talked about what?"

Oh my God.

I can't believe I am going to say this. But whatever. I'm an adult and if I am going to have sex with a man, I should be able to talk about it, right?

Just fucking spit it out, Sisi.

That's what he said.

Shut up, I tell my inner asshole voice.

"Okay, so, we've been a little careless about *protection*," I begin.

"Protection," he repeats.

"Yeah. I mean, um, you know, condoms," I say, and I watch his jaw tense as he grinds his teeth.

"Koukla—" he starts, but I won't let him finish yet.

"Angel, I know we don't have labels for what we're doing, and I am not asking you for anything. I don't expect us to be exclusive. And I realize living here for the time being might be putting a cramp in your lifestyle, but I'm working on that. I've been looking for rooms to rent, and Maria said her old place is still available so I can call the super after I shower," I say, continuing with a rush.

"Giselle—"

"Also," I continue, running right over whatever he was going to say, "I think while we're *intimate* with each other, well, we should start using them. Condoms, I mean. But just so you know, I am on birth control."

I pause, tucking my hair behind my ears, and reaching inside me for a little courage to continue.

"*Also*, I had my last physical at the start of the

summer. Blood work and all, and I'm healthy as a horse. Also, well, I haven't been with anyone but you since way before that, but I know you can't say the same, and, I mean, you understand what I'm saying," I blurt the last, feeling utterly embarrassed.

Seconds stretch between us, and my cheeks are burning. But I don't look at him yet. I can't.

What the hell did I just do?

"Can I talk now?" Angel asks suddenly.

His voice is so deep and even it startles me into looking up. But Angel doesn't wait for me to reply.

He just grabs me by the waist and sits me on his big lap. His hard thighs flex beneath my ass, and I struggle to keep my moan to myself.

One big hand cups the back of my neck, forcing my eyes to meet his icy blue ones, and the other is curved around my hip. Like he is afraid I'm going to disappear or something if he's not holding onto me.

"First, you ain't leaving this condo for some shithole basement apartment with zero security. You are staying right fucking here where I can keep you safe," he says with a finality that brokers no argument.

"Second, demand anything you want, Koukla. Anything. Anytime. Any fucking place. And I'll get it done. I swear it to you. Believe me?" Angel says, and his voice is little more than a growl at the end.

I wonder if that *believe me* is more a demand than an actual question. He raises an eyebrow, and that settles it. I nod, answering him.

Because I do. I do believe him.

"Good. Now, third, if you want me to wear a condom, I will. But I'm clean. I'll send you a copy of my latest physical and you can even talk to my doctor if you want. But there's only been you ever since that first night you tossed a beer in my face. I only want you, Giselle."

"What?"

"I am telling you. I haven't looked at anyone else, Koukla, much less fucked them. There. Is. Only. You."

I close my eyes and a wave of anguish hits me because I want his words to be true. I want to believe them so damn much.

But I know better. And I hate that he's lying to me.

"Stop," I beg him. "You don't have to feed me a line, Angel. I am well aware of your reputation."

"My reputation? Sisi, I'm not feeding you any fucking line. I'm not feeding you anything at all. I promise you'll know it when I do," he says, and the innuendo is not lost on me.

Period or not, I shiver and look down, clenching my thighs together. Angel squeezes my neck, and I flick my gaze back to him.

"I'm not lying," he says.

"The night I left I tried to surprise you at the Den," I confess, finally telling him the reason I ran.

"You came to the Den?"

"Yeah, I did. But when I came in, and I saw you, you weren't alone. A woman was on your lap. She had her arms around your neck, and she looked super comfy. So please, don't lie to me now and tell me that you haven't been with anybody else," I say and now I'm pushing against his hold, struggling to get off him.

But he won't let me go.

"Fuck. I know what you're talking about," he growls, and that's it.

I need to go. I just can't sit there and listen if he's going to explain how he spent the night with that woman. I try to wiggle off him.

"Hang on. Quit squirming," he commands and his grip on me gets tighter.

"You had your say, now let me have mine," he says.

I stop fighting, but I am so done with this shit. I know Angel can see that I'm resigned.

It's right there, shining in my eyes. I blink and two fat tears fall onto my cheeks. And it makes me so angry that I'm crying.

He grinds his teeth. But still, he holds my gaze. Angel doesn't look away. Not once.

"You must have walked in at the same moment Margaret O'Doyle and her new lady, Giovanna, I don't know her last name, came to celebrate her ascension to the head of her family. O'Doyle is an associate of ours. Giovanna, the blonde, is her girlfriend. She was drunk off her skull, climbing onto my lap," he explains, and I am fucking floored.

She's got a girlfriend. And she wasn't hitting on him. She was just drunk.

Ohhh.

"She wasn't making a pass at me, Koukla. I'm not even her speed. But even if she was so inclined, I'd have told her no," he says, and he looks so damn sincere.

"I told you, I only want you."

"Angel," I whimper, thinking about the months in Florida when I probably should have just talked to him.

Am I a fool to believe him?

"I swear I have not touched another woman since you. Don't you get it? I only see you, Koukla."

"Angel," I repeat, murmuring his name.

I whisper because I'm afraid to break this spell. But I'm trembling too, because I want to believe him so damn badly. I just don't know if it's the smart thing to do.

"I know you don't trust me, and now I know why. But I promise you, I'm gonna earn it back, Little Doll. I'm gonna make you believe in me," he says into my mouth as he claims my lips in a kiss that makes me curse Mother Nature.

Angel's kisses are addictive. They're better than coffee and sweeter than ice cream, and I want more. I want to kiss him from head to toe.

Fuck my fucking period.

He kisses my cheek, my chin, and my neck, sucking on that space that drives me absolutely wild, and I swear I could come from that alone. Angel groans, and his tongue laps at me before he licks back into my mouth.

"I still wanna fuck you, Sisi. Period or not. But I can wait till you're comfortable with the idea," he says, plucking at my lips one more time before standing up with me in his arms.

"Get showered and dressed. I'm taking you out

for breakfast," he says and kisses me again before leaving the bathroom.

What is with this man always ordering me around? But the better question is, why do I like it?

I'm in so much trouble.

CHAPTER TWENTY-ANGEL

"Another fucking warehouse has been hit," Nico says, slamming his hands down on his desk.

Images of my Koukla sitting on my lap, whispering my name, flicker through my brain.

"This one is brazen," Luc comments, shuffling through papers as he takes account of what was in our warehouse.

"Yeah, he fucking is. And he's dead. He just don't know it. Angel?" Nico says my name.

The way she melts into me whenever I kiss or touch her.

"Angel?" he repeats, louder.

Shit.

"How much damage we talkin'?" I ask.

Focusing on the task at hand, I compartmentalize. Thoughts of Giselle need to subside for now.

But she's not gone. My Little Doll is always there. Always circling the periphery of my brain.

"Give me a sec," Luc says, and I know he knows what I am really asking for.

It's not about the money for me. It's about how much of our not so legitimate business is gonna take heat for this from the feds.

"Well, the good news is ninety percent of the inventory at that particular warehouse was all legal imports. The bad news is, it's going to cost us about six million."

"What's the other ten percent?" Nico asks, already zeroing in on what I'm concerned with.

"The remaining ten percent are listed as old office appliances and computer hardware."

"Like fax machines and shit?" Nico asks.

"Well, on paper, yes. But we were using some of those machines for storage for our old, *old* books, Boss."

Fuck.

"Was there evidence it was destroyed?"

"No," Luc says, frowning as he continues to read.

"Whoever did this, they stole those old machines before setting the warehouse on fire."

"Angel," Nico says my name.

"On it," I tell him.

And I am.

Whoever this new enemy is, he just fucked with the wrong people. I grab my laptop, and I start going through the feed for that property.

"Most of it is damaged from the heat," I tell them, and I am so pissed.

Whoever this guy is, he's smart. He doesn't want to get caught, and he is covering his tracks.

"What's in those files?" Nico asks.

"My best guess is early affiliations and business deals. It's all coded though, and I doubt he will be able to understand it," Luc says and shrugs. "Nothing groundbreaking, but it's the why that bugs me."

"As in, why is some fuck digging into us at all?" I chime in, and Luc nods.

"I don't know. Maybe he's got a death wish," Nico growls.

He's not wrong.

Obviously, I am going to have to find and take care of this jerk.

But what's worrying me as I read the initial report from one of our guys over at the fire department is that the signature of the explosive device is the same as what was used in Giselle's apartment complex.

"What is it?" Nico asks, and I tell him.

"It's confirmed then," Luc states.

We all look at each other solemnly and I can hear the unspoken order, the silent demand from each of us.

We need to catch this fuck, and fast. I mean that as in like yesterday.

Not because of what he cost us. I mean, six million isn't exactly chump change. But it's hardly going to make a dent in any of our finances.

The building, the warehouse, the inventory—none of that shit is important.

We need to end this threat to keep our women safe. That is the only thing that matters.

Nico looks hard and angry. Luc is quiet, as is his norm. And me, I'm vibrating with the strength of my rage.

This is on me. This man has gotten through my security, and that is not okay.

It falls on my shoulders to see to it this can't happen. Just like I am the one who needs to make it right.

That's fine with me. It's my job. Besides, this guy fucked with my Koukla, and I owe him for that.

He clearly doesn't understand who he's dealing with, which is something that needs correcting.

And I'm just the guy to do it.

CHAPTER TWENTY-ONE-GISELLE

D*ays later.*
The ground beneath my feet is squishy, but I don't mind. I'm wearing thick soled sandals, and the sun is shining.

If my feet get a little wet, it's not the biggest deal. Besides, I am having a wonderful time.

So far, we've watched jugglers, minstrels, and an exhibit featuring birds of prey. A falcon ate a piece of dried meat right out of my hand, and it was amazing.

This is not the kind of place I would have ever guessed a man like Angel Fury would go on a date.

That he would take *me*, of all people, is a whole other category of things I find difficult to believe.

But he did take me, and I am having the best time ever.

"Where are we again?" I ask.

I can't stop my smile from widening as I take in all the stands and people in costumes.

"Tuxedo Park. Haven't you ever been to the Renaissance Faire?" Angel asks, taking a monstrous bite out of a turkey leg that's the size of his forearm.

So yeah, fucking huge.

He offers the leg to me, and I lean forward and take a hefty size bite, too.

I giggle and wipe my mouth with a napkin he hands me. It's weird, but even knowing I just made a pig of myself, I don't feel embarrassed.

I'm a big girl, and I eat. In fact, Angel seems to have this deep-rooted fascination with sharing meals. Lately, he seems to always want to take me out to eat. Sometimes we order in. And sometimes we cook.

The thing I am really starting to love is no matter what we get, he is obsessed with sharing. It's like he's forever giving me bites of his food and vice versa.

And I love it.

It's such a normal couple thing to do, and we are not a normal couple. I don't know what we are.

A week passed since that night at the Den, and ever since then we've been spending every minute together between jobs. I've started up work again, using Angel's ridiculously high-speed internet to connect with my clients.

Figuring out social media algorithms is a passion of mine.

Don't ask.

But I enjoy what I do. Creating content and helping small businesses get their names out means something to me. Sometimes it feels like we're all just shouting into the vast void that is the internet.

With my job, I can make reaching the right audiences a little bit easier for certain people and their brands. Plus, I get to use cool art and design apps.

With Angel spending more time at home and less at the Den, we've been sort of going at it like bunnies.

Well, if bunnies were jacked up monster sized gangsters.

Ironically, I am still not bothered by what he does for a living. In fact, the more I learn, the more I see there is hardly a difference between the criminal side and the legit side of Viper Enterprises.

Angel is pretty keen on the developmental aspects of their legitimate business. It was a surprise to learn he made all the actual renovations inside the condo when he bought Nico out.

"I like to work with my hands," he said, which led to

him showing me what else he liked to do with his hands.

I admit, I am a bonafide fan of Angel Fury's hands.

"Jousting starts in ten minutes. Let's go grab a spot," he says, and takes my hand, moving me in front of him.

He's so big. Attention just flocks to Angel wherever we go, and lately, that's everywhere. It's like he's intent on showing me he wants to be with me.

Angel has been sweet, attentive, sexy, and insatiable.

And, well, I love it.

It's not just the things we do in bed, *and elsewhere*. I mean homeboy is super creative when it comes to fucking.

And I have to admit, I love the way he fucks me.

But this time, it feels different. It's more.

He takes me to restaurants almost every day, or orders in. I offer to cook, but so far, he has yet to agree. It's like he wants to spoil me, and I haven't been spoiled a lot in my life, so I let him.

He rented out an entire movie theater the other night, and he invited Nico, Anna, Luc, and Maria, too. He knows how much I've missed them and he's intent on providing us with safe places to just chill, which really is the sweetest thing ever.

He even had Mrs. Pirillo, Anna's live in housekeeper and part-time nanny, join us so she could have Jr. on hand.

Our trays were loaded with popcorn, candy, and my favorite snack food of all time, movie theater hot dogs.

I might have mentioned how much I like them, and Angel remembered. He remembers everything I say, and it gives me the strangest sensations inside.

Yes, we still go to the Viper's Den. I mean, there is no getting around it. He needs to make appearances there. I know he is not happy about it, but he brings me with him. anyway

I should clarify that by saying he isn't happy about me being around his work. None of the men are when it comes to their women. But this is still new, and he won't leave me home alone.

I don't mind. I like the Den. Always have. It's different this time, though.

No more quickies in his office. No more stolen moments.

I kind of miss that, to be honest, but I am not complaining. Because now, when I get Angel all to myself, he is anything but quick.

He is slow and thorough, and he makes me come every single time. That's not something I've had with any other man.

It's like he is on a one man mission to prove himself, and I am happy to let him.

My entire body is always so attuned to his nearness, so primed for him.

All he has to do is to be here, and it's like my fireworks go off inside every nerve ending.

This date is just the two of us. So, I can't try to convince myself he's doing this to get in good with Nico because I am Anna's friend.

I've had that thought before and it's not one of my proudest moments.

I'm always talking about self-image and how society has tried to brainwash bigger girls into thinking we need to be grateful for any attention that comes our way.

But I never believed in any of that bullshit. And I don't believe Angel needs to suck up to his cousin for any reason. Their relationship seems solid enough without that.

So, why is it so hard for me to accept this big, sexy, powerful man wants me for me? Why is it unfathomable to believe Angel wants me for me?

Maybe it's time for me to shed all that negativity and just go for it.

Dive in, Sisi. The water is fine.

If Angel is the metaphorical water, then he is more than fine. He's fucking perfect. And it's time for me to admit I want him, too. That what I feel for him isn't run of the mill.

I am so sick of playing games.

Angel has given me no reason to doubt his interest in me, and I don't want to pretend I haven't noticed. That I don't want him, too.

Because I do want him.

I want him so badly.

CHAPTER TWENTY-TWO—ANGEL

I know I got shit to handle. Issues to deal with. Problems at work that need solving. Like finding the motherfucker who keeps attacking us.

But not today.

Today, I surprise Giselle with this trip to the New York Renaissance Faire.

It's a weekday, so it's not as crowded as I imagine the weekends are. But after the past few weeks of really getting to know her, I think I have an idea of what kind of things Giselle is into.

This is her first time here, and I feel stupid proud to be the one to take her. I don't know why. But it's something I'm learning to accept.

The emotions this woman conjures from the

depths of my dark soul are things I never felt with anyone else.

Like obsession, devotion, happiness.

Fuck.

I can't stop thinking about her. I want to be with her all the time. Want to see her smile. I swear, sometimes her smile makes my heart stop.

This isn't like me. Taking time off to play hooky isn't something I normally do. My position as Enforcer is demanding. I've got to be conscientious, aware, and on all the time.

I'm responsible for the well-being of a lot of people who are important to me. And it's difficult to turn that off.

But when I am with her, it's effortless. Something about her just attracts joy, puts me in a good mood. That's new.

Hell, that's rare.

It's not that I'm a miserable person, but I suppose you could say I'm a little serious. Not that anyone gets close enough to see that side.

But I'm thinking, I want her that close.

I want to make her happy, because yeah, she makes me happy.

I've been to this Ren Faire before, and as usual, there are loads of people all decked out in costumes.

First thing I did when we arrived was buy her one of those crowns made out of dried flowers with ribbons trailing down the back.

She looks so fucking beautiful. And her eyes haven't stopped darting around, trying to take everything in.

I wonder what she'd think if I took her to Paris, or Rome, or Mykonos. Then I picture doing just that and I know I'm going to someday.

I'll take her everywhere. Anywhere she wants to go.

She giggles helplessly at a couple of male Vikings with huge horned helmets on their heads as they walk past, and I grin along with her. Some people here go all out. They really get into their characters.

While I might not be into cosplay, I appreciate their efforts. And I love watching Giselle as she oohs and aahed over them. Her favorites are the forest of fairies with their brightly colored iridescent wings. But when I offer to get her a pair, she shakes her head.

The joust is about to begin, and I have to admit, it's my favorite thing here. I'm excited to watch it with her. Curious to see what she thinks.

"Here's a spot."

I point to a space on the flat topped stone wall at

the bottom of a small hill. We're smack dab in the middle, facing the fenced off arena.

I watch Giselle frown, and I bite back my grin. My Little Doll is tiny, and the wall is almost five feet high.

She is also wearing one of those long flowy skirts of hers, so I imagine climbing is not an option. Not that I'd let her do that.

My eyes flick to her low scoop neck top, and I clench my teeth. Fuck. She is gorgeous.

"I don't think I can get on that," she says, but I already have my hands on her waist.

I turn her around so she's facing me, and I know the second she registers the heat in my gaze. This woman turns me on so damn hard.

"Hmm. I should have known I wouldn't have to figure it out alone," she replies, grinning as she tips her head back to look at me.

I want to kiss her. But not here. This is a family event and there are a dozen little kids running around next to us.

"Hold this," I murmur and note the shivers skittering up her spine as I hand her the turkey leg.

She takes the perfectly roasted fowl by the foil wrapped end and bites her lip as I squeeze her waist. I can't help myself.

I drop a kiss on her mouth, sucking that lip out from between her teeth, and then I place her on the wall.

"I don't know how you do it. You're always picking me up like I weigh nothing at all."

"Koukla, you're such a little thing compared to me, it is like you weigh nothing at all."

A horn trumpets behind me, and I join her on the high wall, feeding her bites of turkey. I buy a pint of cold hard apple cider from a passing bar wench, and we share that, too.

The joust starts, and it is awesome. Giselle is so into it. She claps and screams *boo* and *huzzah* at all the appropriate places. She waves the little flag I buy from a passing vendor.

Fucking breathtaking.

We are seated in the blue knight's section and the guy wins, which is cool. What's not cool is him tossing his small banner, and a long-stemmed red rose towards Giselle.

I snatch them both out of the air before they reach her. And I glare at that motherfucker on horseback.

"Are those mine?" she asks, but I shake my head.

I hand them to a little girl running past us, and she beams at me and says thank you.

"You don't take gifts or flowers from anyone but me, Little Doll," I tell Giselle, turning back to face her.

I should say something. Apologize maybe. But I hear my girl moan and see the way she's squirming.

Is my Koukla really getting hot and bothered by my very public display of jealousy?

I think she is. And it's making my dick hard.

Even if I'm being ridiculous.

"Come on," she tells me, tugging on my arm.

But I'm still glaring at the knight, and I don't feel her reach for my waist before she gives me a good, hard pinch.

"Ouch! What's that for?"

I'm stunned. This little minx! But I'm also thrilled.

I don't think anyone has ever dared do anything like that to me. And now my pants feel way too tight, and my dick is thumping against my zipper.

"Come here, Big Guy," she tells me, walking us a little bit away from the crowd of people.

She's grinning like she has a secret. And, dirty girl that I know she is, I wonder what she's thinking. She tugs me down so she can kiss me.

And I let her.

"Mmm," I moan, sliding my tongue between her lips. "Now, what is *that* for?"

"That's to say thank you for taking me here," she says.

"You don't have to thank me for that," Angel replies.

"I know. But you deserved a thank you. But this one here is just because I can," she says, tugging me closer.

Giselle kisses me again. But harder this time.

And my response is instant.

I part my lips, snaking my tongue inside her hot little mouth. She wrestles with me for control, but I don't relinquish it. Not this time.

I have one hand caught in her wild mane of hair and the other around her throat, tilting her head back so I can kiss her deeper.

"If you're looking to get fucked in the woods over there, keep kissing me like that, Koukla."

CHAPTER TWENTY-THREE—GISELLE

Angel's promise echoes in my head right before he nips my bottom lip between his teeth. My eyes widen, and his resounding growl tells me he knows why.

It's like he already knows my panties are completely ruined. Soaked through because of his filthy words.

I know I shouldn't like it when he says things like that, but my heart beats double-time and wetness floods between my legs.

"Fuck. Come here," he growls, and pulls me with him.

Excitement sends lightning bolts of awareness shooting through my spine. I've never had sex outdoors.

I mean when would someone like me have that kind of opportunity?

Hell.

I've never even been interested. Never so moved by pure lusty desire that I've ever even been intrigued by the prospect of fucking outside.

Until now.

My pussy clenches. Angel glances at me, his gaze zooming in on my *hard as nails* nipples and I know he can see them through my thin top.

He licks his lips, and now my pussy is aching. I am desperate to have him there.

Inside of me.

I imagine him pushing that big, thick cock of his into me and I moan.

Angel looks over his shoulder at me, and his icy eyes are blazing with heat. You know what I mean.

Like blue fire.

I'm mesmerized by him.

All that worry and precaution I thought I was taking with him this time has all been nothing but hot air. I know Angel holds all the cards, but I don't care.

It doesn't even slow me down. I want him so badly, I'm throwing caution to the wind.

His legs are long, and I am practically racing to

keep up with him. I think we're heading towards the big space where we parked the car, but instead of going towards the gravel lot, he guides me right into the woods.

The sun is setting, and there is just enough light for me to make out his glittery stare.

Angel cups my head and kisses me. I moan and wrap my arms around his neck while he bends, lifting me by my ass.

"Oh God," I whimper as he presses my back against a huge tree.

The hand on the back of my head is stopping me from leaning against the rough bark.

Such a protector.

He takes care of me all the time. No one has ever really done that. And it makes me feel so damn special.

Like I am important to him.

"Hold on," he instructs, his long tongue licking into my mouth.

I feel him working the zipper of his jeans, jostling us both as he frees his dick and rucks my skirt up around my waist.

He pulls my panties to the side and then, suddenly, he's right there.

No pretense.

No warmup.

No foreplay.

In his defense, though, this entire date has been like foreplay. And Angel knows it.

He growls as he kisses me, his big chest vibrating against mine. Then he just flexes his hips, and I-*I love it.*

"Angel," I moan as his big dick pushes into me.

"Shhh. Keep those wild screams for me, Little Doll. Anyone sees you like this and I'll have to kill them."

His words echo in my ears, and I hold him tighter.

God, his words.

They shouldn't excite me. But him saying that, acting all possessive of me, well, it makes me even hotter for him.

"Fuck, you're so wet, so tight," he grunts.

Angel lets go of my waist, and I drop harder, taking his thick cock deeper inside of me.

My nails are clutching at his shoulders and neck. I'm holding him so fucking tight.

His rough breathing fills my ears, and I know he's just as far gone as I am.

It's crazy.

Feeling this way.

Letting him do this to me in public where anyone can see.

But it's also the hottest damn thing I have ever experienced. So freaking sexy. And I know he's telling the truth when he says he'll flat out end anyone who even thinks about peeping.

He feels so good. Holding me like I'm precious. Filling me like no one else. Angel touches me in places I can't even begin to describe.

"That's right, Little Doll. Only I can do this to you. Only me. Feel me. Feel all of me," he growls, and I realize I must have said some of that out loud.

I roll my hips in time with his thrusts, and I do as he asks. I feel *him*. And he is fantastic.

Angel's masculine scent is all over me, surrounding me, and I love it. His big, hard body is more than capable of supporting mine, but I marvel at his strength and the ferocity of his passion.

I'm scared I can't match it, but I do. Pride fills me as I accept the fact that I fit him perfectly. Just like he fits me.

There is no denying this.

No denying us.

I let go of all my inhibitions. Push away all the

nagging reasons I should keep what I feel for him under wraps.

Angel is inside me, so deep. And not just my body. I'm talking about deep inside my heart, my mind, my very soul.

I don't think he even knows or understands at all what I am feeling. And I don't think I can tell him.

Heck, I can't even speak.

My eyes roll upwards, and I see stars peeking out through the canopy of trees.

An owl hoots.

Music from the fairgrounds is still playing. But it's far away. Somewhere in the distance.

I think I hear a car start up, or maybe two, in the lot a few yards away.

But none of that matters.

All that matters is this.

Him.

Me.

The present.

My orgasm is building, and building until it crashes into me, washing out every other sensation. I bite down on his neck, trying to muffle my moan.

It's too much.

It's not enough.

Angel is wrecking me. He is destroying me for anyone else.

The way he's been courting me.

The way he touches me.

How he makes me feel.

He's becoming everything to me. And it's not enough. I still want more.

I shouldn't trust him. I shouldn't want him so badly.

But I do.

God help me, I really do.

His huge cock strokes inside me again, curving just right so he's hitting my G-spot, and my orgasm doubles.

My orgasm drags on. He feels so damn good. It's all too much.

Clinging to him, I know I can't keep quiet.

He knows it, and he presses down on the back of my head, fitting me firmly to his neck, and I bite harder.

I worry I'll hurt him, but this is Angel. He likes it rough, and he rewards me by grinding against my needy throbbing clit.

Angel's moves become jerky as he follows me right over the edge.

"That's it. That is fucking it. Suck the cum right

from my body," he growls, and I feel his cock pulsing as he fills me with his hot seed.

There's so much of it. It's dripping down my thighs.

"Fuck. You're so fucking good at taking me, Little Doll. So perfect," he says, and his breathing is rough.

Angel pulls out, reaching between us, he scoops some of the mess from between my legs with his big hand, and he shakes it onto the forest floor.

Then his hand is back, and he's fixing my panties, petting my pussy when he is done. And I shouldn't like that. It's absurd.

But I do like it.

"Such a good girl for me, aren't you?"

Angel smiles, and he kisses me sweetly. Another reward for a job well done.

I melt into him, sighing when he allows me to slide down his body.

He keeps me steady with his big arms wrapped around me, and I'm grateful. I need a moment before I can stand on my own.

"You good?"

I nod.

"Yeah, you're good," he says it with pride this time. "So good and dirty, aren't you, Little Doll?"

I bite my lip. He grips my neck, pulling on my hair as he tugs me closer.

"Let's get you home and clean so I can dirty you all up again. Want that? Tell me."

Excitement hums in my veins. I swallow, my eyes never leaving his as I open my lips to respond.

"Yeah, Angel, I want that."

It's the truth. I do.

CHAPTER TWENTY-FOUR-ANGEL

I fidget with my phone, glancing at the screen for updates.

Giselle is at her parent's apartment, checking in on Resa today. Her sister called and told her she and her boyfriend had the flu or some shit.

Koukla is such a fucking sweetheart, she made a big pot of soup herself and insisted on bringing it over.

Warmth rushes through me as I picture her taking care of me like that.

It's weird. I never had that. But I want it.

I am so fucking obsessed with this woman.

Still, I worry. I was supposed to go with her, but then I got called in for a meeting. I wanted to tell her no. But that would be crazy.

I might be obsessed with the woman, but I'm not crazy. So, instead of me, she took six heavily armed bodyguards with her. My top guys.

It's the only way I can bear to let her out of my sight. Especially after the news I get at this meeting.

"The aftermath of taking Sanchez down is turning into a problem, Boss," Luc says.

"How so?" Nico asks.

"Small time players thinking about taking over. They don't seem to realize it's ours now," Luc says.

He's talking about Ghost. It's the codename for a Chinese gangster who runs everything from drugs, guns, gambling, and girls from Connecticut to New York City.

He doesn't have a foothold in Jersey, but he wants one. Mainly, he wants our ports.

Like everybody fucking else.

Criminal organizations like his are like cockroaches around here. You stomp on one, you got a thousand more waiting in the wings.

Luc starts citing off eyewitness reports from our eyes in the field. His guys are pushing their boundaries, taking over turf that ain't theirs.

The Vipers don't deal in petty shit anymore. And what we allow, we allow because we have the final say.

We don't allow trafficking of any kind in our city. As for drugs, well, the best we can do is keep dealers out of schools and parks.

People are gonna do what they want. But some shit is pure poison, and we keep that out of our city.

Every day it seems drug laws are changing. I don't do them myself. But I don't judge others.

The Vipers might not be boy scouts, but we are a damn sight better than other motherfuckers out there. Those guys don't care if their junk is killing people.

"Two people were found dead last night in the alley behind the Iron Cage," Luc says.

The Iron Cage is a bar about ten minutes away from the Den.

"So what?" I ask, because unfortunately, dead bodies aren't exactly hard to come by in Jersey City.

"So, they OD'd. They both had empty baggies with a G emblem on them."

"Fuck," Nico growls.

"Ghost. It has to be," I tell them.

No, Ghost hasn't been a problem for us before, but without Sanchez around, the illegal drug market is down one major player.

It's possible the Asian gangster thinks he can fill the void.

A thought he is likely to regret.

I am already texting one of my team leaders to scope out the motherfucker's known haunts.

If Ghost needs a message from the Vipers just to be clear that this town is off limits, he'll get one.

And soon.

"On it," I interrupt Luc, and the Council dips his chin.

"Good. Now, let's talk about our new agreement with Margaret O'Doyle," Nico says.

"She's got balls," Luc replies. "Already she's dismantled the prostitution ring her sleazebag father was involved in and put those who wanted jobs to work for her."

"I bet that was shocking for a lot of people," I say.

"Yeah. She's really turning that old Irish mob family into a female-strong organization."

Luc grins. I just grunt. Margaret O'Doyle is smart and daring, but she is young and inexperienced. A lot of folks won't like what she's doing.

"How are the boys taking it?" Nico asks, and he's smirking.

My cousin always liked rooting for an underdog, but if there is one thing I learned in our dealings with the new head of the O'Doyle clan, it's that Margaret O'Doyle is smarter than people think.

I guess that's what makes her the perfect dark horse. She's a twenty-two year-old woman who's already established she won't take shit from any man. Not even her pops.

That piece of shit had to go.

But his redheaded firecracker of a daughter coming out as bi and slaughtering half the original members of her old man's organization?

Well, that's just sheer audacity. Margaret O'Doyle is ballsy. I will give her that.

By inviting the Vipers to her ascension as head of the O'Doyle clan, she is proving smart.

Very fucking smart.

Because Margaret O'Doyle is telling the whole fucking world who she's in bed with.

Metaphorically, of course.

None of us are touching anyone but our women ever again. We know it. And for the most part, they know it.

My Koukla needs some assurances, and I'm gonna give them to her. I was planning on it this weekend, but now we have to go to Boston, and I'm hoping she is okay with it.

"Alright, here's what Ms. O'Doyle is offering us to officially partner up with her," Luc begins, and yeah, I know I should be paying attention, but

I'm not.

My mind is elsewhere. Specifically, it's back in my condo where I left Giselle this afternoon, all spent and sweaty. Sprawled out across our bed, the sheets in a perfect state of dishevelment at her feet.

Our bed.

Fuck.

I really like the sound of that, but the woman keeps bringing up looking for her own place like she thinks she can't stay with me.

I want her to.

Can I do that? Can I just keep her?

I mean, I don't see the problem. But the woman avoids the topic like it's got cooties.

Even without the sex, and let me tell you, the sex is fucking incredible, we get along. I enjoy talking to her, laughing, watching movies, taking her out, spoiling her. Even cooking together is a good time.

The things that come outta her mouth. Jesus Christ. She is so goddamn delightful. I mean, she thinks about things I never even considered.

She's smart. Like really smart. Curious about everything. And she is not afraid of a fucking thing.

Not a big oaf like me, that's for sure.

I *like* her. I really like her.

Shit.

That sounds stupid. But I think it might be important.

I know Giselle isn't some stray kitten I picked up off the street. And no matter how badly I want her to stay with me, I am going to have to give her more than I have been.

Shit.

My feelings aren't something I talk about very often. I mean, I'm the head Enforcer for one of the most formidable gangs in the tri-state area.

I don't exactly wax poetic on the regular.

But if it means keeping her with me?

I'm willing to try. And isn't that a fucking stunner?

Of course, we're beyond attracted to each other. I can't keep my fucking hands off her, and just thinking about it makes me hard.

Hell, she's just as insatiable as I am. And it's sexy as fuck.

"Angel," Nico interrupts my wayward thoughts, and I flick my gaze to my cousin's.

Luc's already left the office, and I didn't even fucking notice.

"What?" I ask.

"Boston. It's this weekend."

Fuck. I forgot all about that.

"This weekend?" I repeat, but I know my cousin didn't fucking stutter.

"You got a problem with that?" he asks, and the fucker is smirking at me.

"No, Boss. No problem."

The king can be a real ass sometimes, but no, I don't have a problem.

I just need my girl to come with and for the weekend to go smoothly.

Easy fucking peasy.

CHAPTER TWENTY-FIVE-GISELLE

After spending an entire day doing my sisters' and her asshole boyfriend's laundry, cleaning the mess they made of the bathroom and common rooms, I finally leave them with a pot of homemade soup and all the over-the-counter medicine I could find.

"Ready, Miss Vega? The boss is waiting for you," Banks, one of my new plethora of bodyguards asks me as I gather my things.

"Yeah, we can go," I tell him.

Resa and Dan were inside the bedroom, sick as dogs, so they only saw one of the guys come inside with me.

"Oh my God, are you dating like a politician or a rap star or something?" Resa asked.

Of course, I didn't explain a thing to her.

What could I say, really?

My boyfriend, who I'm not really sure if he is actually my boyfriend because we don't use labels even though I am living with him, is involved with one of the most powerful criminal organizations on the eastern seaboard?

No biggie.

I roll my eyes. But I didn't have to explain. I gave her and Dan some electrolyte infused water and a couple of cold and flu tablets and they fell asleep within minutes.

The cleaning part I did on my own. Just thinking about our parents seeing that mess made me cringe.

They won't be returning to New Jersey for a couple of months yet, but still. I plan on having a talk with Resa when she is feeling better about all this.

I tuck it away for now.

When I get back to the apartment, I see Angel feeding Buffy a plump mouse, and I have to fight not to shiver.

It's just nature, and the snake is only doing what snakes do.

"Koukla," Angel murmurs the nickname he has for me.

He dips his head towards the kitchen, and I follow him inside, where he washes his hands.

"How's your sister?" he asks.

"Oh, she is sick as a dog, but she'll be fine," I tell him, and I'm ridiculously pleased he asked.

He dries his hands. Next, he's reaching for me, and I go to him willingly.

"Kiss me, Koukla. Make my day better," he tells me, and I feel so warm all over.

I do as he asks. I kiss him, and I hope he feels even half of what I do.

"That's my girl," he whispers, dropping another kiss on my lips before leaning back.

"Hungry?"

"A little," I tell him. "I made a chicken salad with the meat from the soup. We can do sandwiches if you want."

"Sounds perfect."

We make our simple dinner side by side and Angel puts together a tomato and cucumber salad with veggies from Luc's garden to go with it.

To say I am shocked that Luc has a garden is an understatement, but the salad tastes wonderful, so I keep those thoughts to myself.

"I'll take care of the dishes. Why don't you take a bath and relax?"

A bath does sound amazing, so I don't fight him on that. I just go.

My eyes are closed, and I'm leaning back in the enormous tub when I hear the door open.

Angel is standing there, and he's staring at me like I am the best thing he's ever seen. The water is clear.

I didn't use any bubbles or anything, and the lights are on, so I know he can see everything. Typically, I'd be covering up or yelling if anyone walked in on me naked. But with him, I don't feel self-conscious.

All I feel is anticipation. And I am right to feel that because Angel is coming closer.

He's taking off his clothes as he walks, and it's like my own private male revue.

I sit up, and my chest is rising and falling with the increased pace of my breathing.

Holy shit.

He is so beautiful.

"Beautiful? I think that might be a new one," he says and grins, shucking off his pants.

The black boxer briefs can barely contain his hard cock, and I lick my lips.

Angel's physique is beyond impressive. He's six and a half feet tall, but even without all that extra height, there is the fact he has more muscles than any man I've ever seen in person.

His entire body is covered in ink, except for his chest. The thick, scrolling artwork is expertly done. So sexy. I never know what to look at first.

Next, he's bending down, his eyes on my tits as he removes his boxers.

Holy. Fuck.

His dick is thick and long and there's a drop of precum forming at the tip of his mushroomed head.

I know what I want. But I've never done this with him before. And I don't know how to tell him.

"See something you like, Little Doll?"

I nod and Angel fists his cock. He walks to the edge of the tub, and I am already on my knees, practically drooling for him.

"Fuck, Koukla. Are you sure? You want to give me your mouth?"

"Yes, oh yes, I am sure," I say.

Then I close my hand over his, and I tug him forward by his dick.

I place my lips around him, and I moan as I finally get a taste of my Viper.

"Fuck. Your mouth is so hot, Sisi. You feel so fucking good."

I take him deep as I can and tears sting my eyes as I gag. He is so big, I can't help it.

I look up, expecting him to be upset or something, but he's not. He looks, damn, he looks like he is holding on by a thread.

"That's it. Relax that throat, Koukla. Take me deeper. I know you can," he encourages me.

His big hands cup my face, and I do as he says. I relax. Angel moans loudly, flexing his hips and sliding that big dick down farther.

I scrape my teeth against his velvety skin, and he hisses. He pulls out, waiting for my nod, and I blink as more tears fall.

"Again," I say, and I open wide.

"Fuck. Yesss," he hisses, and this time I get him about three quarters of the way down.

I lick and suck and scrape as I use my mouth on him, and he, well he seems to like it.

His hands tighten in my hair as he rocks his hips.

"Shit. So good. I'm gonna come soon," he tells me and tries to move me off him.

But I don't let him.

"Koukla, you can stop now," he says, but he's groaning.

I like the sound of it. I like that I'm the reason he's making those sounds.

I can stop now. But I won't.

I want him too badly. Want him to lose control like he makes me every time he touches me.

My pussy throbs and I snake one hand down my belly, Angel's eyes go wide as he watches. His growl is back, and it's like the vibrations are going straight to my core.

"Goddamn. You gonna touch yourself while you suck my dick? You're so turned on with your mouth on my cock you can't wait for it, can you?"

Angel moans and grunts, and now he's the one fucking my mouth.

I rub my clit in circles beneath the warm bath water, my sex so needy I can't even think straight.

He pushes my head down harder and pulls out, leaving just the tip inside my mouth. Angel shouts, his whole body is going stiff, and I rub myself faster.

I am so damn needy, but I can't seem to get there. I want to scream my frustration, but my mouth is full of dick, so I can't.

I'm stuck. Floating, just hovering really, right on the edge of carnal bliss.

Then I feel something warm inside my mouth and the second I feel it hit the back of my throat, *finally*, I start to come.

"Fuck, Koukla, are you squirting for me?" Angel

growls and his question makes me drop my gaze to the floor, where his is currently pinned.

Pleasure roars through my veins, and yeah, it's all over the floor, too.

"Goddamn it, you are so fucking sexy. Gonna make you do that again. This time all over my face."

His words are so filthy, but they make me feel so damn sexy.

And he makes good on his promise.

Angel sits me on the edge of the tub and he licks into my cunt until I squirt again. He makes me come so hard, it drips down his chin.

And it's even better than I hoped for.

CHAPTER TWENTY-SIX-GISELLE

Holy. Fucking. Shit.
  I squirted.
Twice.

I didn't even know I could do that. But maybe it's just because of him.

Duh.

It is definitely him.

I know he's ruined me for anyone else. And it scares the shit out of me. So I push that thought away and I focus on the present. On the now. And how good he makes my body feel.

I won't think about my heart. Or the fact I am dangerously close to being in love with him

I can't.

Deny. Deny. Deny, Sisi.
It is the only way I know to survive this.

CHAPTER TWENTY-SEVEN-GISELLE

After our dirty little bath, Angel drops a bomb on me.

He has to go out of town on business, and he wants me to come.

I should say no. It could be dangerous. But I know Angel would never put me in harm's way.

I don't know how long this thing is going to last before he gets bored. And the truth is, I don't want to be away from him.

The ride to Boston is fast, but Angel always drives like a bat out of hell. Only this time, he's not driving.

It's Banks. He's one of the bodyguards who was with me at my parents' house.

I recognize he's one of Angel's top and most

trusted men. He never looks directly at me.

In fact, none of his men do, and I appreciate that.

They are all big and hulking, though none more than Angel. I'm getting used to the fact these men are all armed and dangerous, and honestly, it's not as weird as it should be.

I don't know if that means I'm becoming desensitized or if it never really bothered me to begin with.

Angel's been working on his laptop for most of the drive, but he still manages to ask me if I need to stop or if I want something to drink.

"No more of that," he mutters and turns off the laptop, quickly depositing it back in the leather bag beside him.

I think it's a Tom Ford, but I'm not sure. It's sleek, expensive, and really fucking nice. But Angel always has good taste.

I fidget with my outfit. We are going straight to this black tie event, and we stopped about half an hour ago to grab a snack, shower and change.

With the evening traffic, there's no time to go to our actual hotel first, and I'm grateful Angel had the forethought to make the arrangements.

The Boston address we're headed to is about five hours away from Jersey City, give or take. Sitting in a gown or a tuxedo for that long wouldn't have been comfortable for either of us.

Angel is always thinking about my comfort. Something I really appreciate about him. He exhales and closes his eyes for a moment.

I take the time to check over my dress and I cover my belly with my hand and wonder if this was the right choice.

Anna and Maria helped me pick it out. It's something I borrowed from Anna's closet since I have nothing fancy enough for a black tie event in my meager selection of clothes that survived after my apartment was blown up.

That reminds me. I need to go shopping.

But if I'm being honest, well, I wouldn't have had anything to wear to something like this, anyway. And since the party was kind of short notice, this is fine.

I'm a little taller than Anna, but other than that our body types are very similar. Now that she's still breastfeeding, our boobs are even the same size, so the bodice fits me perfectly.

It's a dream of a dress. An off-the-shoulder confection with capped sleeves and draped pleats on the bodice and waistline. The skirt is long and there is a little train. The side slit makes it easy for me to walk.

I never wear this color. But the navy blue is pretty, and for some reason it brings out the green of my eyes.

I was going to iron my hair, but I veto that. September weather is fickle, and I can't be sure it won't rain.

So, I leave it loose and curly instead. Angel likes my hair, and the truth is, I keep it down for him.

Both the cut and color of the gown are flattering, and I should feel quite confident. But I'm so nervous, and I am aware Angel hasn't looked at me once.

Leo follows the line of cars up a long driveway, stopping outside of an enormous brick mansion. There are several men and women with weapons. Security, I assume.

"Wait for me, Koukla," Angel murmurs as the car comes to a stop.

I do as he asks, watching him prowl around the front of the black luxury vehicle. He is always handsome. But tonight, seeing Angel, *my tall, muscular, tattooed lover*, in a midnight black tuxedo is almost too much to bear.

Holy. Christ.

I don't know who named him, but Angel is the

right moniker for this man. Not because he is a saint or anything. More because he is brimming with masculine beauty.

He looks like he was chiseled from marble. Like something that should be in a museum.

I swallow nothing and freeze when he opens the door. The first thing I see is his big, inked up hand outstretched towards me, and I don't have to think.

I just take it.

I place my hand trustingly in his and I allow him to pull me out of the car. The skirt parts, and Angel's eyes go right to the flash of thigh that peeks out from the long slit.

Then I grin.

Because he isn't ignorant of this fantastic gown or how it looks on me. He's simply avoiding it, and I think it's because he can't take it off me yet.

Yes. Please.

Knowing that he wants me like that is like the strongest aphrodisiac ever. My skin warms, and my mouth goes dry all at the same time.

They say knowledge is powerful, but I never knew how right they were until now. Because that knowledge, well, it sends my heart thundering inside my chest.

Angel Fury wants me.

Me.

Giselle Vega.

And I know it. And knowing it is power.

"See something you like, Big Guy?" I whisper as I stand in front of him.

His icy blue stare pins me, and he leans forward, crushing my lips against his.

I feel his tongue pressing against the seam of my lips and I am so fucking glad I chose to not wear lipstick.

He kisses me long and hard, and in front of the dozen or so other guests lining up to get in. It feels like more than a kiss. It feels like a proclamation.

Angel kisses me with pure possession, and I revel in it. I want it.

His dominion over me.

His brand all over my skin.

Whatever you want to call it, I want it.

I want Angel Fury to claim me. I keep dreaming of the time I can finally say I belong to him. And he belongs to me.

Just that.

I've never had that. Never belonged to someone and the desire I feel for it is bone deep. I want to be able to say it out loud.

Love me. Please. Love me like I love you.

I make the wish silently, moaning softly as he slows the kiss. He presses his forehead to mine and I breathe him in.

"Yeah, Koukla, I see something I like. But I don't like anyone else seeing it," he tells me with a possessive note that sends a flood dripping between my legs.

"They just get the wrapping, Angel. What lies beneath it is all for you. Only you," I tell him, and place my hand on his chest.

My man rumbles and fuck, it is so sexy. He takes my hand, kisses my knuckles, and tucks it in the corner of his arm before guiding me to the entrance.

We don't wait in line. Angel walks right to the front and the couple there steps back. The older man looks worried when Angel glances at him once.

But he doesn't need to do more than that. Security is waving us through, and I don't spare the other people another thought.

I'm here with Angel Fury and his presence is palpable. The man oozes power and strength. Other people, well, they recognize it. And they bend to it.

Nico is the King, and Luc is the Council. But Angel is the Enforcer.

He is the hammer of justice in everything the Vipers do.

He is vengeance and retribution.

He is devastation and annihilation.

And he is mine.

Pride and possession fill me as I straighten my shoulders and allow him to lead me inside. We walk through a long, elaborate hallway to a room set up like some kind of gala event.

I don't really understand what we're here to celebrate. But I don't care. I get to be with Angel, and this man makes my knees knock and my pulse race.

"Come on. We need to say hello to the guest of honor."

"Okay. How long are we staying?" I ask, and I look up at him through heavy lidded eyes.

Angel looks good enough to eat in his crisp white shirt and black tux. Several heads turn to stare at the big, tatted up man, but he doesn't spare any of them a single glance.

His glacier blue eyes are zeroed in on me, and I feel special.

I feel seen.

Chosen.

I feel lucky to be with him.

That's so messed up, Sisi.

But I ignore my inner voice. Angel is a handsome man, and he is powerful. He can have his pick of women. But here I am. Lucky that this tall, sexy, powerful man has picked me.

Even if only for a little while.

Yeah, it's gonna hurt when he realizes I'm no match for him. But for now, I'm gonna grab onto what we have for however long we have it. I'm going to cling to him with both hands tight.

He makes me feel so damn good. It's a high I've never felt. One I'm beginning to crave.

It's reckless. Thoughtless. And I am not a fan of the whole *YOLO* thing, but *YO* fucking *LO*.

If I only live once, I wanna live as much as I can with him. Angel isn't good in the traditional sense. He's dangerous. Maybe even scary. But he makes me feel so damn good.

No other man has ever made me feel this way.

Oh shit.

My head is swimming and my pulse races like a pack of hounds chasing a rabbit.

Fuck. I'm so stupid.

I did the one thing I should never have done. I've gone ahead and given my heart to him. And I am realizing it all right now as I stand there frozen in Angel's stare.

I'm in love with him.

He cocks his head to the side, measuring his

thoughts before he answers the question I've just asked and already forgotten about.

"Only an hour. But I promise to twirl you around the dance floor, take you outside on the terrace overlooking the rose gardens, then I'll kiss you under the moonlight," he says, and I swoon.

My panties are ready to just melt off my body. Angel's grip on me tightens, and he speaks low this time.

For my ears only.

"After that, I'm gonna take you back to our hotel room, strip you out of that gown you've got on that's making me crazy, then I'm gonna fuck you until you come screaming my name. I won't stop till you see stars, my dirty Little Doll," he whispers and my heart squeezes so tight it's a wonder I don't pass out.

"Angel!" a shrill voice interrupts us, and thank God, because honestly, I'm halfway to coming just from his words.

The woman is stunning, and familiar. My heart tightens inside my chest. I recognize her.

It's her.

The blonde I saw him with the night I left Jersey City for my parents' condo in Fort Lauderdale. The woman I thought he was cheating with.

I know now there was nothing going on, but still. I tense.

She is coming in hot and she looks like she's going to try to hug him. But Angel is quick, and he's smarter than people give him credit for.

With one arm already around me, he moves so both arms encircle me, and his shoulder is ready to intervene should she try to make contact.

The woman has no choice but to halt in her tracks. And I exhale slowly.

"Ah, well, hello again, Angel," she says, stopping her attempt to hug my man. "This your date? Hello, I'm Giovanna."

"Hello Giovanna," Angel says, but his tone is cool. "This is my—"

"I'm Giselle," I say, interrupting whatever he was about to say.

I know it's silly, but hearing him say the word *friend*, or even *girlfriend*, right now might actually make me cry.

I know, I know.

I am being dramatic, but I can't help it. I finally admitted I am in love with the man. Even if only to myself.

And I get it. It's my fault. My baggage. Completely on me.

My brain knows better than to love him. But my heart, well, my heart is a free spirit and loving him is the only thing that makes sense.

But the thing is, I wish, well, foolish as it is, I wish I was something more to him than a temporary thing.

"Okay. Well, it's nice to meet you, Giselle. And let me say, *wow*, that dress looks stunning on you! Come on, let's go say hello to Maggie," she says, ignoring Angel and taking my hand.

I step out of Angel's protective embrace to shake hers, but she starts dragging me along with her instead. I turn and see Angel frown, but I can't just pull away from this woman.

It would be rude. And I think she must be a friend of the Vipers, or at least the other woman, *Maggie*, is. So, I just go with her.

Angel is following us, so I don't worry too much about it. His expression is thunderous, but since that is his default, I have no idea what he's upset about.

I walk along with Giovanna as she passes through throngs of people eating appetizers and drinking frosted shot glasses of dark liquid.

Whiskey, I believe.

I take one as I pass a server and toss it back. Giovanna shouts in approval and I giggle.

I don't usually drink in strange places. But I'm with Angel. And really, I need some liquid courage.

I don't really know what tonight is about, but it looks like my cousin's wedding did a couple of years ago. There's a bunch of people I don't know, lots of food, drinks, and questionable music.

Everyone is decked out in their best, and I am glad to see I match the vibe. Angel, of course, is better looking than anyone else there. But that's to be expected.

"Well, Giselle, are you ready to meet the guest of honor?" Giovanna asks, winking at me.

I don't know why my hackles are raised, but they are. Still, I smile and nod at her. What choice do I have?

CHAPTER TWENTY-EIGHT-ANGEL

My name is Angel Fury. Emphasis on my surname.

Yeah. It's mine.

Some people think we made it up, Nico and me. But we didn't.

Our family has a long history, and one of our great-aunts or something spent years tracing our roots back all the way to ancient Rome. She wrote a whole book about it, but it's in Greek and I never got around to getting it translated.

Yiayia, our paternal grandmother, was born in Athens. She came to the states like most people during World War II from Greece.

Yiayia was quite the lady. She raised me after my parents died.

Oh, she was tough and loving. When Nico's mother died of an overdose, how she wept for her daughter-in-law.

I am older than Nico, and maybe I remember things a little differently. Like the way she spoke Greek more often than not. It didn't matter my mother was a mix of Italian, Irish, and Puerto Rican.

I was just like a million other people in this neck of the woods. The son of immigrants. A mix of all the rich cultures and ethnicities in this part of the world.

But to Yiayia, I was hers, and that was all that mattered.

She told me stories of where the name Fury came from. And I ate them up. Nico did, too.

The original three Furies are, of course, the daughters of the goddess Gaea. They deliver divine retribution, vengeance, raining justice on those who displease the gods.

It's something we talked about often when he, Luc, and I started the Vipers. If you believed the stories, then our heritage is soaked in violence and vengefulness.

Coming up on our own was a long, grueling battle. But together, we did what we set out to do.

We took over the neighborhood, and ever since then, we've been expanding.

Maybe our corner of the world is better for it. Maybe to some it's not. But I don't worry about that.

The point is, I am a Viper.

Lethal.

Cunning.

Powerful.

And full of fucking venom.

I don't trust Giovanna. The blonde woman has a sneaky sort of aura about her. And I really don't like her manhandling *my* woman.

Still, I won't cause a scene here. Not yet, anyway. I just follow where Giovanna is leading my Koukla.

My thoughts stray, and I think about the way Sisi tensed right before Giovanna reached us. How she was probably recalling seeing the skinny blonde on my lap.

As if I wanted her there.

But I understand why Giselle jumped to the conclusions she did, no matter how off base they were.

And I get mad.

I think about how my Little Doll cut me off from calling her mine when I made the introductions.

And that increases my ire.

I don't like that. Not one bit.

If Giselle tries to deny my claim on her by ignoring it, then I am going to have to do something she can't ignore. Something no one can refute.

My pulse is racing, but my eyes are wandering over her supple body in that fucking dress and I grind my teeth.

The thin fabric does nothing to hide the sway of her plump ass as she walks, or the rise and fall of her magnificent tits that is inevitable with every breath she takes.

It's not her fault. She's built like a goddess. And I love how she looks.

But she's mine to look at. No one else's.

I think about how Nico killed a man for looking at his woman, and I wonder if it's possible to clean up an entire fucking ballroom full of bodies because if I catch one more person's gaze on my Koukla for longer than is acceptable, I might just kill every last motherfucker here.

Then, I wonder what she might think if she knew all this. Giselle doesn't know how I feel, the insane thoughts rattling around my head, because I keep that shit close to the chest.

But so does she, I realize. She doesn't tell me everything she's thinking, and I want her to.

That sort of thing only comes with trust.

I can make her trust me. Believe in me. All I need is time.

I wonder if maybe my Koukla is having the same thoughts I've been having for days. And I have been having some seriously deep thoughts.

But maybe she's also wondering what to call herself in connection with me.

Now, I'm mad at myself.

But I'm not sure what the solution is.

Saying she's my *girlfriend* isn't enough. I'm forty fucking two years old. I don't have girlfriends.

And if I did, Giselle is still more than that.

She's my, my—*she's mine*.

The women stop walking and I narrow my eyes, deciding once and for all. After tonight, Giselle is going to know without a doubt where she stands.

I take two enormous steps, and I grab her arm, yanking her back none too gently from Giovanna's loose grip.

"Ah, I see how it is," the blonde says, and I don't like her smile.

She might think she's untouchable because of her connection to Margaret. But that means shit to me.

I don't smile or joke. I simply tuck Giselle against my side and feel her sigh as she leans into me.

"Angel, I am so glad you're here," Margaret's booming voice interrupts us.

The redhead is the new leader of the O'Doyle clan, thanks to the Vipers' interference, and she's coming towards me with one arm extended. Her other arm is wrapped around a tall, thin man with a shock of white hair slicked back from his face.

I'm not familiar with him. And I don't like that she's bringing him close to my Koukla.

I turn my body slightly, so Giselle is between both my arms. I don't smile. I don't even acknowledge him.

The message is simple.

She is mine.

She is protected.

And she is off fucking limits.

My face is like fucking stone, and I don't move a muscle. I watch silently as Giovanna leans against Margaret's other side.

"Angel, I want you to meet John Chen. John, this is *the* Angel Fury," Margaret says and smiles, and she looks like the cat that got the canary.

Fucking shit.

I know what this is. It's a flex.

Margaret O'Doyle is showing off her connection

to the Vipers. To impress her girl, or maybe this stranger, I don't know.

Maybe she thinks she can play this game now because she's a boss.

But she can't.

Not with the Vipers.

And most particularly not with me.

I don't play games.

Margaret says something flippant, but I ignore her. I don't want to start anything here. So, I refuse to engage.

"Angel, you were so much more fun when we visited the Viper's Den," Giovanna says, and she eyes Sisi like she's got some secret or something.

I feel my woman tense, but I squeeze her neck unobtrusively and she settles.

That's my girl.

But now they made Giselle uncomfortable and I'm getting annoyed.

"Giovanna, play nice. Apologies, Mr. Fury, but I am so thrilled to make your acquaintance," the stranger says.

I look at the man, John Chen, and at his extended hand and I don't blink.

I have one hand on the back of Giselle's neck and

the other on her hip. Releasing her to shake this man's hand is not something I'm inclined to do.

So, I don't. John Chen raises an eyebrow and offers a quick bow.

"A pleasure, I'm sure. How are you enjoying your evening?" he asks with no trace of an accent.

He looks Asian, but I'm guessing he grew up right here in the states. Hell, for all I know his family has been here longer than mine.

I don't answer because I don't know him. And when his gaze flicks over Giselle, I accept I don't need to know him. I just need him the fuck away from me.

My blood boils. I don't know what the fuck Margaret is trying to pull tonight.

Maybe Luc and Nico are right. Maybe she's a good fit. Ready to take over.

Or, more likely, little Miss O'Doyle is not ready for this responsibility.

But it's still not my business. Giovanna is cuddling up to John now, but the fucker is still looking at my girl.

It's not her fault. Giselle is a fucking knockout for sure. Truly, his aren't the only eyes to stray her way tonight.

But he's closer than those other fuckers. And his stare is lingering way too long.

The grip I have on my inner monster is starting to slip. I stand up straighter, pulling his attention back on me.

"Apologies, Mr. Fury, for staring. Your wife looks simply stunning tonight. You are a lucky man," he says.

"Oh, thank you, but we—" Giselle starts to speak, but I apply some more pressure to her neck, and she closes her mouth.

"What brings you here, John?" I ask, ignoring his comment.

It's better if I focus on why he's there and not the way he talked about Giselle's appearance.

Motherfucker.

Focus.

Suspicions swirl around my brain, and none of them are good.

"Oh, Margaret and I are old school friends, aren't we? Of course, I am here to celebrate her ascension to the throne, as it were," he says and Margaret smiles at him and nods.

But her smile is brittle.

It doesn't reach her eyes. Giovanna is grabbing a

shot of whiskey from the tray of a passing server, and I notice her smile is gone, too.

What the fuck?

Something isn't right. And I am sick of all the pretense. But this is how the game is played. I have to bite my fucking tongue for now.

"I see," I say, and offer one more nod before making our excuses.

"Perhaps I might have a dance with your wife," John says, and if it wasn't for Giselle's tight grip on my arm, I swear I might hit this fucker.

I exhale and ignore him. Again.

"Congratulations, Miss O'Doyle, on your new promotion. But I promised my wife this dance. Excuse us," I say, my eyes meeting John Chen's once more before he looks away first.

I turn to walk away, placing Giselle just in front of me. I don't let go. My hands are on her, one on her elbow, the other at the small of her back.

I have to process everything that just went down, but right now all I can think about is how she froze when I said wife.

Something inside me stirs at using the word where she's concerned.

I never imagined I would be the type of man to

get married, but as I lead us through the crowd to the dance floor, it's all I can think about.

"Why did you say that?" she whispers.

The dance floor is crowded, but people move out of our way, creating space. I take Giselle in my arms and finally, my inner monster starts to calm.

The music continues, and I start to move with her.

"Why did I say what?" I ask, and I drag her closer.

She's tiny. Short. But I love the way she fits inside my arms, and dancing with her is nice. More than nice.

It feels right.

"Wife. Why did you call me wife?" Giselle asks, and I don't like the look in her celery green eyes.

She looks fragile. Like she'll crack if I say the wrong words.

"Because he assumed it, and I don't know that man. It's safer if they think you are my wife," I tell her, and it's not a lie.

It is safer.

But it's not the only reason.

Fuck.

I should just tell her the truth.

But old habits die hard deaths. And I'm not Chatty fucking Cathy when it comes to my feelings.

Truth is, I never felt this way about anyone. I'm not sure what it is. I mean, is it love?

I don't know. I've never been in love with a woman before.

Just say it, you weak fuck, even if only to yourself.

My inner voice is a cocksucker, but I ignore him, focusing instead on my Koukla's pretty gemlike stare.

The sparkle that's been there all night dimmed a little at my explanation and I don't like that.

I want her happy again. I want her glowing.

The DJ is playing something slow and romantic, and that's fine with me because all I want right now is to feel her in my arms.

"Did I tell you how gorgeous you look tonight?" I ask.

It's true. And it's the right thing to say. Giselle's smile is so bright it rivals the sunshine as she tilts her head back to look at me.

"Actually, you didn't, and I was wondering if maybe I chose the wrong dress," she replies, biting her lip coquettishly.

"Nothing wrong with that dress, Koukla. You look like a fucking goddess, but it ain't about the dress. It's just you," I tell her right before I lean down and claim her mouth.

That fucking mouth.

If anyone asked me what my favorite part of a woman is a year ago, I'd say something stupid. Like her tits. Or her ass.

And don't get me wrong. Giselle has fantastic tits, and her ass is divine.

But it's her mouth that gets me every fucking time.

The things she says. The sounds she makes. The way she tastes.

Fuck. Me.

I fucking love her mouth. I'm obsessed with it.

With her. I love her.

Emotion sizzles through me, and I am so fucking amped. I know I said we'd stay an hour, but I've had enough of these people and this place.

I want to be alone with my woman.

My Little Doll.

I want to peel that gown off her smooth skin, touch her softness, test how wet she is for me. I want her juices dripping down my chin, soaking my balls as I fuck her hard and deep with nothing between us.

After that day we talked about protection, I sent her copies of my most recent physicals. I'm fucking clean and I know she is, too. She hasn't mentioned it again and I'm glad.

Of course, if she insisted, I'd wear a condom. Hell. I'd wear two. But the fact is I don't want a fucking thing between us when we make love.

Or fuck.

Or whatever.

Shit.

I guess it is making love. Even when we fuck.

I can say it now. Because I love her. I'm wild about her.

Giselle completes something in me I didn't know was missing. But now that I have her, I don't want to know what it feels like to be missing that piece ever again.

Wife.

I called her wife before, and it felt so fucking right. The more I think about it, the more I want it.

Her.

As my wife.

I need to keep her with me. I plan to.

If I have to fuck her into submission to walk her down the aisle, I will. But I think maybe she wants me just as much as I want her.

Is it possible she loves me?

She's looking up at me now, her peridot eyes

glowing and my chest squeezes. I don't know if she loves me or not.

But I want her to. And I can help her get there.

"Fuck this. Let's go."

I stop dancing and take her arm, dragging her towards the door.

"Where are we going?" she asks breathlessly.

I look back at her and see her grinning, and I know she's excited. I can fucking feel it throbbing in her veins.

"Remember that promise I made you before?" I ask, and her cheeks turn pink.

"Yes, Angel. I remember."

Goddamn.

I have to stop to adjust my dick. Giselle whimpers, and fuck, I feel my cock get even harder.

"Angel," she whispers, and I feel her need inside the dulcet tones.

It dances across my skin, snaking up my spine until it wraps around me like a vise.

I love it when my Koukla says my name.

But tonight, I'm not stopping until she screams it.

CHAPTER TWENTY-NINE-GISELLE

The hotel room is dark when we get there, and Angel doesn't bother with lights. He walks me backwards until I feel the wall behind me and presses his big body up against mine.

"Turn around, Koukla," he commands.

And I listen. I can't help it. I want to obey him.

I feel Angel's callused fingers on my back as he works the zipper down, dragging the beautiful confection off my shoulders as he works.

Anticipation dances over me, making me shiver and ache. The gown falls to the floor, and I am left standing in nothing but my heels and sheer panties. It had a built in bra, so I didn't have to wear one underneath.

A fact I am grateful for as Angel cups my bare

breasts from behind before coasting his palms over my belly, waist, and ass.

"So fucking sexy," he growls right before I feel his mouth on me.

He bites my neck, then laps at the abused skin with his tongue. I gasp when I feel him drop to his knees, pulling on my hips so I am leaning against the wall, my ass thrust out.

"That's it, Little Doll. Gimme what's mine," he grunts before pulling my panties off.

"Open," he commands, and I spread my feet apart wider, worried my arousal is now dripping down my thighs.

Angel is so close to where I want him, but his fingertips just keep teasing my inner thighs and calves. Never quite getting to where I want him.

Frustration makes me whimper, and I hear his deep chuckle.

"Easy, Koukla. I got you," he growls, then pushes his face between my cheeks.

I can't help myself, I moan when his tongue snakes across me from my soaked entrance to my asshole.

He eats me with vigor, and I can't do anything but hold on to the wall and let him.

"I love it when you come on my tongue," he growls as he stands up, taking me with him.

Somehow, he's managed to hoist both my legs on top of his shoulders, and now he is carrying me, holding to him with his large hands on my ass.

"Now I wanna feel that pussy flutter around my dick," he grunts as he drops me onto the bed.

I bounce, but I don't have time to do more than grab onto the comforter for some semblance of stability. He bends down to kiss me, just as ferociously as he ate me, and fuck, the taste of my pleasure on his tongue is more than I can handle.

My heart is hammering inside my chest. Too soon, he breaks the kiss and Angel grabs my ankles. He stands up at the foot of the bed and drags me to the edge, so my ass is almost sliding off the mattress.

I'd likely fall to the floor if he wasn't blocking the way. But he won't let me fall.

I know he won't.

He puts both my legs on either shoulder as he grabs his dick and lines it up with my slick slit.

I know I haven't really asked him any of the relationship questions I should have asked. I know this is reckless, and a little careless.

But I also know no one makes me feel the way

Angel does. So, when he rams that thick cock between my legs and fills me up so I don't know where I end and he begins, all I can do is take it. And take it.

We both groan when he bottoms out, and fuck, this feels good. He feels good.

"Goddamn. You're always soaked for me," he murmurs and drags his cock in and out of my channel at a punishingly slow pace.

"Angel. Please," I beg.

I am too far gone to care about the state of feminism or how I reek of desperation when he's plowing into me. I can't give attention or credence to anything other than how he feels inside me.

And he feels fucking fabulous when he's inside me.

"You take me so good, Little Doll."

His movements increase, his dick hitting home with every slide. But he doesn't stop there. Angel reaches between us, he circles my clit with his big, callused thumb.

"Oh, God!"

"Not God. Angel. Say it. Say my fucking name."

"Angel," I moan.

He moves faster. His thrusts are harder. His

thumb is still working me over. My pussy squeezes. I feel it happening. Then I scream because he's making me come so hard.

"ANGEL!"

"Fucking yes, Koukla. Come all over my cock. Show me who you belong to," he growls, dropping forward to cage me in.

He lifts a knee and pushes his way onto the bed, moving me up the mattress with his freakishly powerful muscles. He swivels his hips, grinding himself against me.

It's so good. It's all so damn good.

Angel wraps his big hand around my throat. His icy eyes are locked on mine. And his dick never stops moving inside me.

"One more. Gimme one more," he commands.

My mouth drops open in a silent scream as what was one orgasm becomes two.

I'm vaguely aware of Angel's movements getting staggered and sloppy, right before he arches his back and spills himself into me.

"Mine. You're all fucking mine," he growls, collapsing on top of me with his mouth against my neck.

I don't know how long we stay like that. But it's

perfect. I simply wrap my arms around his massive body, loving the feel of his weight.

I close my eyes and breathe him in because he is right.

Yes, I am his.

For however long he wants me, I'm his.

BOYS

CHAPTER THIRTY-ANGEL

"I can't believe that little brat," Nico says, shaking his head.

I am telling him and Luc both what went down in Boston. Relaying the little power flex, Margaret O'Doyle tried to pull.

"Have you found anything on this John Chen character?" I ask Luc.

My guys managed to snap a few pictures of him at the party. It's not much, but it's enough to run facial recognition software or to match it against any records that might pop up.

"Nothing," he says.

"And you said he went to school with Margaret, but I've combed through all the registered attendees of her schools from preschool through college, including dropouts and transfers, and there is no John Chen anywhere."

"So, who is this guy? A fucking—"

I lock eyes with Nico right before we say it at the same time.

"Ghost."

"Goddamn it, Angel! You had him right fucking there," Nico snaps.

"I had no way of knowing who he was, boss," I reply through gritted teeth.

"Fuck. I know!" Nico yells and slams his hands on top of the desk.

I pace back and forth. I'm so fucking mad. And not just because I had Ghost right fucking in front of me, but because he saw Giselle.

My Koukla.

And the motherfucker made remarks about her.

Luc is already on the phone, calling Margaret. But the newest head of the O'Doyle clan isn't answering. Giovanna does instead. And what she says isn't comforting.

Not one fucking bit.

CHAPTER THIRTY-ONE-GISELLE

"Girl, I know you aren't moping around after spending the weekend with Angel in Boston," Anna says as she changes Baby Nico's diaper.

"It wasn't a weekend. It was one night. Oh, and I'm sorry I'll have your dress replaced. It sort of got torn," I mutter, and my cheeks burn pink.

"Torn? How? *Ohhh*. Never mind," Maria says.

I cover my face with my hands.

"Get it, Sisi! Now, don't worry about the dress. Oh, here, hold Jr. while I throw this out," Anna says, and hands the baby to me while she gathers his dirty diaper up and wraps it in some smell-blocking biodegradable trash bag before tossing it into the bin.

"Wait. I want to know more about this whole Boston trip. Including the dress ripping part!"

Maria is mixing some non-alcoholic cocktails at the small bar in her magical fucking library that Luc basically gave to her before they got married.

I swear, she is one lucky bitch.

Ever since Luc sort of claimed her at the bar, she's been his. Like Anna and Nico. But things didn't work out the same for me.

So yeah, I am moping.

I mean, Angel is great. But I don't think he's into commitment. And I don't think I can settle for less.

"I don't want to talk about it, Maria," I tell her, and I make goo-goo faces at Nico Jr., who is just about the prettiest baby I ever saw.

"Hey, how did you get hold of the precious one?" Maria asks, setting the tray with our drinks down as she makes a grab for him.

"No way. You had all this little guy's attention when I was away. It's time for him to bond with Auntie Sisi, now," I say, refusing to give him up.

"Baby hog," she snipes.

"You bet your fat ass I am," I tease.

Anna comes back towards us, shaking her head, and the three of us burst out laughing.

"You're both going to spoil him rotten. But, um,

FYI, you aren't going to have to fight over holding him for much longer. There will be one for each of you," she says, biting her lip and her cheeks are bright red.

"What are you talking about?" Maria asks, sipping her drink.

I take a sip of mine and I moan in pleasure. I don't know how she does it. But she's made some sort of fresh fruit punch soda mocktail and it is fantastic.

The fact she serves them with brightly colored silly straws just makes me love her even more.

"Oh my God! You're pregnant?" I shout, and Anna is nodding and crying, holding her hand over her mouth.

"Yeah, I am."

"Again? Anna, how does this keep happening to you?" I ask, equal parts happy and surprised.

"Well, Sisi, when a daddy loves a mommy very much, he puts his penis inside her, and—"

"Shut up!" I tell Maria and shake my head at her.

"You guys, I know it's soon, and the doctor said as long as I was breastfeeding, I should be fine. But um, either I have like bionic eggs or Nico has super sperm, cause here I am, knocked up again," she says, and her lip is trembling.

"Hey now."

"Come here."

I join Maria with baby Nico in my arms on either side of Anna. We have this group hug going on and we're all sniffling by the time we're done.

"Did you tell him?" I ask.

Anna is already nodding.

"Yeah, of course. He's the first one I told. And he's so happy. He says he can't wait to watch the whole thing this time from day one. Then he kissed me and held me all night, and in the morning when I lost my breakfast."

"*Lost your? Ew!* You have morning sickness already? That's not something people made up?" Maria asks, scrunching her nose.

"Oh no, it is very real," Anna says, and talks about how sweet Nico is with her.

My mind wanders as they talk about the early stages of pregnancy, but I am only half-listening. I wonder about children, and if I will ever have them.

Does Angel even want them? Would he want them with me?

The fact is, I'm not sure and I don't know how to approach the subject. I mean, hell, we still never cleared up the whole him calling me wife in public thing.

"Okay, I don't think we are going to get to talk much about the book we've been reading, but I am excited to tell you all, Luc and I made a date to celebrate our wedding. Since, you know, we got married in the freaking hospital," she mutters, but her smile is wide as she starts detailing their reception.

"It's going to be so beautiful. Oh, I am sorry. It's these damn hormones," Anna says, and yes, she's crying again.

The baby falls asleep in my arms, and I put him in his little playpen, careful to clear the toys out of the way.

"Okay, now that we got all that out of the way, we want to know what is going on with you," Maria says to me.

I look from her to Anna and back again.

I've known Anna since I was a kid, and Maria might be newer to our circle of friends, but she is just as important to me.

They are both waiting expectantly for me to confide in them, and really, I want to.

"Look, I know I have nothing to complain about. I am an adult, and I am the one who makes all the decisions for my life."

"Has Angel been bullying you?" Maria asks, and she looks furious.

"Bullying me? Oh my God, no not at all. It's just. Well—" I heave a sigh.

I'm so confused about me and Angel and it's so nice to have someone to talk to.

So I do. I talk to them.

I tell them how I saw Angel with a woman who turned out to be the girlfriend of the new head of this Irish mafia family. I tell them about how I ran to Fort Lauderdale to create distance, since he obviously wasn't into me like I was into him.

"Which we know is bullshit cause he came to get you," Anna says.

I roll my eyes at her, but I continue with my story.

I tell them about how before I went to Florida, we only ever met at the Den and had sex in his office. We never went out or anything.

But when we came to get me, he's been different. Taking me out. Letting me stay in his condo.

"Which I thought was your condo at first, by the way. Way to trick me," I say, narrowing my eyebrows at Anna.

"In all seriousness, Sisi, your apartment got blown up. And who is gonna fuck with Angel Fury's condo?" Anna says and I have to agree with her.

"Um, look, I am sure Angel is crazy as the rest of

them when it comes to your safety," Maria starts, "but you know that isn't the only reason he is keeping you at his place, right?"

Anna and I both just look at her.

"Guys, Angel never dates anyone. I mean, women used to throw themselves at him all the time. I worked there seven months before Anna came around and Luc and I became a thing and, in those months, I never saw him leave with a single one of those women."

"Are you trying to say Angel was a virgin? Cause we know that ain't true," I say, trying for humor when all I feel is a desperate urge to believe her.

"I swear, Sisi, not one woman in all that time."

"So you mean, you think he cares," I whisper, not daring to say it too loudly.

"Oh my God, girl. *Cares?* I think he's head over fucking heels," Maria says.

"Yep. That man is insanely in love with you. And if he's not, I'll just have Nico take him out," Anna tells me, and I think she's kidding.

But with Nico. Who knows?

"Oh my God, Anna! That's one of the things I'm scared of. What if he's just trying to fit in with the other guys by doing whatever this is with me?"

"That's it. I am not listening to this bullshit from

you. Sisi Vega, you are one of the best people I know," Maria starts.

"And you have the biggest mouth of anyone I know, so," Anna adds, side eying Maria who nods.

"We both think you need to get your head out of your ass and tell the man how you feel."

"What?" I say, completely shocked.

"Just walk up to him. Take his hand," Anna says.

"Or his dick," Maria adds, and shrugs when Anna gasps at her.

"What? I mean, whatever is going to work to get his attention, am I right?"

"Okay," Anna concedes. "Walk up to him, take his hand, *or his dick*, and say *Angel, I need you to know how I feel*, and then just tell him."

"Tell him what?" I say, exasperated.

"Girl, tell him you love him. Then see if he loves you, too."

I feel tears rolling down my cheeks, but I don't wipe them because they are right.

I do love him. And I am not a coward by nature.

It's time for me to pick my big girl panties up and tell him.

Gulp.

CHAPTER THIRTY-TWO-ANGEL

My phone buzzes and I glance down. I am not expecting any calls, but when I see it's from my Koukla, I am all smiles.

KOUKLA

> I'm about to leave Maria's. I just texted Banks to pick me up. But I wanted to ask you what time you'll be home? Will you be there for dinner?

I close my eyes and lick my lips. It's not the first time she called the condo *home*, but whenever she does, I get this ache in my chest. I know I need to make it official. And I plan on it.

Tonight. I am going to ask her to be mine for real tonight.

ANGEL

> Wrapping things up. Banks is picking up Buffy from the vet. He'll be there in six minutes. Then it's fifteen to the condo. I expect you to text me in exactly twenty-one minutes that you're home.

KOUKLA

Wow. Crazy much?

ANGEL

> I need to know where you are at all times, Little Doll. Nonnegotiable.

KOUKLA

Why don't you just track me then?

I don't answer.

KOUKLA

Oh, my God. Do you track me? Angel! Seriously. That's crazy.

ANGEL

> I am crazy about you, Koukla. Now, stop asking questions if you don't want the answers. The car will be there in two minutes. Wait for him to pull inside Luc's garage before you leave the house.

KOUKLA

(three dots…but no reply)

> ANGEL
>
> Tell me you understand.

> KOUKLA
>
> Yes. I understand you. Sheesh. I guess this means you like me.

> ANGEL
>
> He's there. Get your ass in the car and lock the door.

> KOUKLA
>
> Yes, Angel.

My heart pounds harder and all my attention is on her. I watch that little dot as the car drives away and my chest feels so fucking tight.

I think about those weeks when we were apart. I think about her taking off now. And suddenly, I can't fucking breathe.

She can't do that again. I won't let her.

No way this woman is ever getting away from me.

Not now. Not ever.

I am keeping her.

For good.

CHAPTER THIRTY-THREE—GISELLE

"Goodnight," I tell Luc's security guard before I get in the back of the black SUV I arrived in earlier.

I always beat the other guys to the door, not liking it when anyone besides Angel holds the door for me.

That's the first mistake I make.

The second is I am still texting Angel when the car starts to drive away, a smile on my face.

But something is wrong.

I look up and I see I'm not alone.

"Banks?" I say, but the man driving is not the same bodyguard Angel always assigns me.

The man sitting across the bench from me is

vaguely familiar. There's a carrier between us, and I recognize it as the one Angel uses to transport Buffy.

Oh. Fuck.

I try to avoid that animal at the best times, but on checkup days especially. She tends to get cranky when she's in the car.

"How nice to see you again, Mrs. Fury," the man says, and that's when I place him.

It's John Chen. The man I met in Boston. Only his hair isn't slicked back, it's spiky like he's some punk rock star.

"Mr. Chen. What are you doing here?" I ask, turning to face him.

I hope like hell I am pressing the correct button on my cell phone before I let it slide to the floor.

"Well, I've been trying to get the attention of your husband, but the Vipers are tough to get an audience with."

"Oh, well, I am sorry about that. I can pass along a message for you," I offer, but the man starts to laugh.

I really don't like it. He sounds off. Like his laughter comes from a place of madness rather than mirth.

"It's too late for that, Mrs. Fury."

"Um, where is Banks?"

"Your driver? I imagine he is traveling across the veil as we speak."

"Traveling? Oh my God. You killed him?"

I gasp. My heart squeezes. Banks and I weren't like pals or anything. But I liked him. And Angel must have known him for years.

I hurt for him. For my Angel. Then I close my eyes because it's the first time I think of him like that.

My Angel.

It doesn't matter if he claims me or not. I claim him, and that counts, too.

My beautiful avenging Angel.

He will come for me. I know he will. And I tell this asshole that because I believe it with all my heart.

"You understand by doing this you are signing your own death warrant, right?"

"Ah, well, Death comes for us all, I'm afraid. Now, give me the phone you dropped on the side of your seat."

"I didn't drop anything."

But I stop speaking because John Chen is pressing an enormous gun against the side of my head.

I whimper. But I reach for the phone.

"Good," he says and speaks into the phone.

"Mr. Fury, I have your pretty little wife. I will call you with a location when we can meet and talk. We have a lot to discuss."

He doesn't hit end. The man I know as John Chen, but who I think might be that Ghost I've heard Angel mention, opens his window and tosses my phone out to be crushed to bits on the road.

"There now, Mrs. Fury," he says, and that's when I feel a pinch in my leg.

I look down and see this crazy fuck is holding a syringe. Panic makes me choke on my words, or maybe it's whatever he gave me. I feel numb and tingly, and all I manage is a gurgling sound before I slump against the seat.

John Chen, or Ghost, or whoever he is, turns to me with that horrible, empty smile on his face.

"Why don't you just settle in? This is going to take a while."

I want to run. To scream. To anything.

But I can't move a muscle, and even though I want to stay awake, I can't. Fear is still coursing through me, but right before the darkness takes me, I have one thought.

Angel is coming for me.

I know he is.

That thought is the only thing that calms my speeding pulse.

CHAPTER THIRTY-FOUR-ANGEL

The second my phone connected I was on the move. I caught only the first minute of my Koukla's call and I became aware of two things, two definite things, immediately.

Someone took what's mine.

And I'm going to kill him for it.

"Mr. Fury, I have your pretty little wife. I will call you with a location when we can meet and talk. We have a lot to discuss."

This motherfucker.

"Don't you fucking touch her," is all I manage to say before all I hear is wind followed by the sound of glass breaking.

Fuck!

Fury like I've never known fills me and I am already taking off, running down the hall as I call all my available men to me.

"We gotta go!"

I slam open Nico's door. He's in a meeting with a dangerous-looking man in an expensive suit.

I shouldn't be interrupting him, but I have no choice. My cousin doesn't question me. He just stands and grabs his guns from the cabinet next to his desk.

Luc is in there with him, and he does the same.

"Sorry, we have to finish this another time," Nico tells the man.

But he grins wickedly, joining us on this little off road adventure.

"Family is all that matters. Please, allow me to lend a hand," the man says, and I place him then.

This is Adrik Volkov, the billionaire and former Bratva crime lord.

There have been whispers about the *wolves of Volkov Industries*, and I know enough about them to discern that this man's morals align with the Vipers when it comes to our women.

It's one of the first things I discovered when I vetted the man before we even considered entering a partnership with them on this real estate development project Nico and Luc were cooking up.

Adrik Volkov has a fucking army at his disposal, and I am too fucking worried about my Koukla to refuse his help.

I nod my head, and he grins. It's not a nice smile. But it is familiar.

The monster in my soul seems to recognize the one in his and vice versa.

"Excellent. Let's go hunting," Nico replies and claps his hands together.

We're already in the car by the time I get everyone up to speed.

"How are we going to track them if he dropped the phone out the window? I assume he also disabled the car's GPS and tracking systems?" Adrik Volkov asks.

That's when I turn to face him, grinning like a wildcat.

"Buffy."

"Buffy?" he asks, and he is looking at me like I am crazy.

"That's right. Buffy had an appointment today at the herpetologist's lab," Luc says.

He laughs.

Nico joins him.

And Adrik mutters something in Russian.

The car that took Giselle is approximately thirty-five minutes ahead of us, but I'm breaking every traffic law to catch up.

Hold on, Koukla. I'm coming for you.

It's a promise I mean to keep.

CHAPTER THIRTY-FIVE-GISELLE

"Get up."

An unfamiliar voice is talking in my ear and the next thing I know, someone is slapping me across the face.

"Ow! Okay, okay," I respond and stumble as I am yanked out of the car.

"Hold this," the same voice says and thrusts something at me.

I open my eyes and try to catch the carrier as Chen pushes it into my hands.

Buffy is heavier than she looks, and I stumble under the weight of the thing.

"Um, please," I say, shaking like a fucking leaf.

"Afraid of a little python?" Chen laughs, and so does his driver.

I don't think they know what kind of snake Buffy is, and I don't know if it's important or not. But it might be.

Trusting the snake to stay inside the thing, I rearrange it in my arms and follow the driver while Chen aims a gun at my back.

"Keep walking. Good. Now wait," he says.

And I do. I have no choice.

It's still light out, but I know it is later in the evening. The sun doesn't set until around eight or so, but even with the diminishing light this place looks familiar.

We pulled into the back of an enormous brick house and are headed inside what looks like an old-fashioned double garage that sits behind the main structure.

"Inside," Chen orders, and I have no choice but to obey.

Ten minutes later I am tied to a chair in the middle of a room and Buffy, the poisonous black mamba, is at my feet in her travel tank.

The driver is guarding the door, holding a very large, deadly looking gun, and Chen is on the phone.

I don't understand what he's saying. It's not English, but I don't recognize the language either.

A few minutes later, I see someone approaching

the door and I narrow my gaze. She looks familiar too.

Holy. Shit.

I know where I remember this place from. We're in Boston. At Margaret O'Doyle's house.

"What the fuck, Chen? You brought her here!" she yells.

"Why?" I ask her. "Why did you betray the Vipers? You know what they'll do," I tell her, mad as hell that she had a hand in this.

Angel doesn't share a lot about his business with me, but I know this woman is considered an ally. Maybe even a friend.

I don't know what makes a person like this betray another, especially a fellow woman, but I know it won't go unpunished. And that mollifies me just a little.

"Shut up," Chen steps forward, cursing under his breath.

"You know I'm right. They are going to come for you both," I tell him, and this time he slaps me harder.

"Shit, Chen, She's right. They aren't going to back down and now they'll think I had a part in this!"

"You do have a part in this, Maggie mine," someone else says.

Chen turns around to face the direction of the voice, and he is smirking. I'm still seeing stars over that last slap, but I recognize the silhouette of the woman as she comes into view.

"Giovanna?" Margaret says, sounding confused. "I don't understand."

"What's there to understand? I used you to get an introduction to the Vipers. That was all I wanted you for. Now, you're useless to me," Giovanna says, raising a gun.

"You work for her, don't you Chen? And you, you're the Ghost!" I say suddenly putting it all together.

"Brava! Give that girl a cigar!"

Giovanna grins wickedly, turning around like a runway model.

"You're Ghost? Wait. What do you mean? I thought you and I—"

"What? You thought that was real? Oh, Baby, you're so green. I wonder if Nico put you in charge just so he could manage you."

"Fuck you. Now, where's my brother?" Margaret yells, and I see tears well in her eyes.

Her brother?

If Ghost kidnapped Margaret's brother, and was posing as her girlfriend, gathering intel, then shit, this whole thing is a complicated web of betrayal and backstabbing.

But it explains her part.

I think of Resa and everything I would do for her. It makes sense.

Angel will still be pissed, but I can't blame her. I understand Margaret O'Doyle's motivation to betray the Vipers. But not Giovanna's.

Buffy hisses inside her tank, and I look down at her. The lid on top of her travel tank rattles and I look down, my fear growing and not because of the guns in the room.

Angel has told me enough about her to know that an agitated black mamba is not something I want near me.

"Please, enough with the drama. Baby boy is fine. He's tied up in the other room. You can have him back, Maggie mine, but not until I say so," she says, then hits Margaret in the face with the butt of her gun.

She shouts in pain, then drops to the floor. She just crumples like a pile of old clothes. And my fear level rises.

"Now, how is our little victim?" Giovanna says in a mock baby voice before stopping in front of me.

This bitch.

"I am not a victim," I snap, angry at this woman for not only toying with my life, but with all of us.

"Not yet," she says and smiles.

Giovanna is not a nice woman. I knew that before. But when she touches me, wrenching my face up with her nails digging into my chin, I want to vomit.

"What's so special about a fat little nothing like you that Angel Fury would turn down a chance to fuck me?"

"Maybe it's because I'm not a heartless bitch," I spit the words at her.

She squeezes my face tighter, and I feel warm liquid dripping down my chin. I think this bitch cut me with her nails, and now I am even madder. The rattling at my feet intensifies.

I watch Giovanna raise her hand, she is lifting the gun to my temple.

Shit.

I know Angel is on his way, but he won't get here in time. Sadness wells inside me. Sadness and regret.

I should have told him I love him. Should have said it every day.

Chen and the driver are dragging Margaret's body off to the side.

One of them leaves and goes inside the other

room, returning with a young man who is either dead or unconscious.

Chen is bent over, tying Margaret's hands together. And it looks so much like a classic mob movie. The kind where they line up their enemies and shoot them before leaving town.

This bitch is going to kill me. And I don't want to die like this.

Hell.

I don't want to die at all. But if I am going out, I am going to do it my way.

"Any last words?" she says, moving back a step and taking aim.

"Yeah. Catch!" I shout just as I kick open the loose lid on Buffy's tank.

The blank mamba is in a vicious mood. I've seen it before. I know when she is ready to strike. And as Giovanna looks down to see what I set in motion, it's too late.

Buffy launches herself, the venomous serpent is in full on attack mode.

The snake bites her several times, and Giovanna screams, her gun, forgotten, drops to the floor. It goes off, hitting one of her guys. The driver, I think.

Chen is yelling, but I am too busy pushing myself back, away from where Giovanna is struggling to breathe. She is on the ground now and her face is grossly distorted. A side effect of the venom.

I am looking around frantically for Buffy, but I don't see the snake.

"Where is it?" Chen shouts and lifts his gun.

But before he can start shooting, the garage doors bust open and there he is.

My Angel.

Three steps and Angel slices Chen's throat with a wicked-looking blade. His eyes are glowing with rage, but that changes when he sees me and charges across the room.

Other men follow him, but I don't pay attention. My focus is on him alone.

"Koukla. You hurt? You okay? Fuck. I got you," he rumbles soothingly as he cuts my binds and pulls me into his arms.

Angel hugs me tight as I sob into his neck.

"I'm sorry. Giselle, I'm so fucking sorry. I failed. I should've protected you better," he says over and over again, holding me so tight, repeating himself.

But I don't understand. He didn't fail. He saved me. He got here in time.

"You crazy man, you did nothing wrong."

"I did. I fucked up. I'm sorry. Please say you'll forgive me. Don't leave. Please don't fucking run again, Koukla, please. I can't stand it. I can't fucking live without you. Just give me another chance—"

He's rambling now, but he's saying things I never imagined a man like him would ever say. My heart squeezes tight, and I know I can't let him think like this. I can't let him hurt.

Not now. Not ever.

"Angel," I say his name.

I cup his face between my hands, loving the rough feel of his five o-clock shadow, then I pull him to me for a kiss.

"Koukla?" he whispers, kissing me one more time.

"I forgive you. You did nothing wrong, but I still forgive you."

"You do?"

"Of course, I do. I love you, Angel. I'm not going anywhere."

The air between us feels charged. I smile at him through my still falling tears, and it's not a coy grin or flirty little tease.

It's a full blown smile. And it belongs to him.

Just like the rest of me.

"I'm gonna spend the rest of my fucking life making you happy," Angel says and picks me up, hugging me tight.

"You damn well better," I tell him, laughing when he spins me.

"Fuck! Snake!" someone shouts, and Angel turns around.

He's still not letting go of me, but I'm not complaining.

"Oh," I tell him, watching with no small amount of amusement as a bunch of beefy men rush outside the garage because of one tiny little snake.

Buffy is a badass, though, so I am pleased they are giving her the proper amount of respect.

"You should probably get Buffy back in her tank," I tell him, and his shocked stare meets mine.

"Buffy?" he says and his gaze flicks back to Giovanna's dead form.

I glance away the second I see her swollen, discolored face and the horrific expression that is still frozen on it. A result of suffocating to death.

It's gross. And not something I want to remember, so I close my eyes.

"Wait here. I'll get Buffy."

I nod and turn around. It takes Angel a few minutes, but with the help of a garden rake, he gets his pet viper safe and sound, secure in her tank.

"I'm building her a whole new habitat when we get home," he says, and I grin.

"How about we move it to your office? I mean, I love this little girl, but I'm thinking she might be happier in the Den with the other Vipers."

"Good point," Angel agrees.

He gives me a wink and a smile, and my heart almost beats me to death. He hands Buffy to one of his guys, and then Angel turns back to me and wraps his arms around my body.

"Let's get those scratches checked out. Make sure you're alright. Then I'm taking you home. That okay with you?"

"Yes, Angel."

And it is okay with me. Truly, one hundred percent, okay.

EPILOGUE ONE-ANGEL

It takes an hour and a half to clean up the garage and make it like nothing bad ever happened there.

Nico and Luc stayed behind to get Margaret O'Doyle's full story, but I heard enough to agree she's not a hundred percent to blame.

But some of it is her fault, and she needs to be punished. Liam, her kid brother, is just out of high school. He's young, but apparently gifted with computers and technology.

He's going to work for us as payment for his sister's misdeeds. She fucked up by not coming to us when Ghost started making demands.

But I get it.

She thought Chen was behind everything, when

really, she was being manipulated by her lover. Giovanna was actually Giovanna DeMarco, the daughter of a former mafia hitman who ran to China after giving up his crew to the feds.

Snitching ain't good for anyone in this business.

Apparently, old man DeMarco led his daughter to believe his family had betrayed him by giving territory to the Vipers.

That was her beef.

She thought we bamboozled her father and got him sent up the river.

But that's not how it went down.

The DeMarcos were already losing ground when Nico, Luc, and I were up and coming. Sure, we took over their business, but that was after he ratted out his players and ran off.

I had to hand it to her though, I never suspected Ghost was a woman, much less Giovanna.

When I think about how she kidnapped my woman, I get so mad.

It's more than anger. More than rage. Fury is the only word to describe it.

I wish I was the one to end that bitch's life. But I can't say I'm not proud of my Koukla for her fast thinking. Proud and terrified.

If we hadn't gotten there, Buffy might have bitten

her as well. And that is not something I want to dwell on.

Seems my Little Doll is a snake charmer, and I don't just mean Buffy. She's charmed the fuck out of me, and I am hers.

Solely and completely hers.

I just need to get this ring on her finger.

"Stop fidgeting, bro," Nico says, grinning as he fixes the collar of my tux.

Giselle likes me dressed up. So, instead of running away to Vegas like I wanted, we're all dressed up like a bunch of fucking penguins, waiting in this enormous old church for my Koukla to walk down the aisle.

"Is it hot in here?" I mutter.

The AC is on, but I am starting to sweat.

"Take it easy. Maria said she is on her way," Luc tells me.

I grunt and nod my head. I look around the church. It's nowhere near full, but that is because of me. My one stipulation was that the crowd be small for security purposes.

I don't have much family left. Just Nico and Luc and their wives, and the baby. But they are all in the wedding party, so they aren't sitting down.

I wonder if Delia is pleased with the gift I sent her. My new mother-in-law is something else.

She loves saying things like *there's an Angel at my table* whenever I visit. I have to admit, I don't mind it.

I can see where my Koukla gets her big heart from.

Anyway, I had a diamond pendant shaped like angel wings made just for her. A special thank you gift for welcoming me into her family with open arms.

For my father-in-law, I sent him a set of engraved golf clubs. I don't play, but I thought he might like them along with a lifetime membership to that country club he likes to frequent in Fort Lauderdale.

I know I don't have to buy their approval. Hell, it's not like I would just leave my Koukla if they didn't like me. But I want them to like me, so I am making an effort.

Three dozen of my men are serving as security, and they are strategically placed inside and outside the church.

Giselle's family takes up six rows on the bride's side. And that's just her immediate family.

Her mother and father are with her, as well as her sister, Resa.

Her jerk of a boyfriend, Dan, is sitting with the rest of their family. I'm not a fan of Dan's and I plan on letting him know real soon.

The little prick squirms when I glare at him.

Good. He should know who the fuck I am and what I'll do if he steps out of line.

But I'm not thinking about that right now.

I breathe in deep, letting the different smells around the altar filter in. I smell incense and flowers, but beneath that is that apple pie cinnamon goodness I associate with my bride.

She's here, but I can't see her yet.

I feel a sense of warmth surrounding me, and I think of Yia Yia.

Would she be happy now? Proud of me?

I think she would be. Giselle has the same spunk and spontaneity my grandmother had. Also, the same loyalty and zest for life. I think Yia Yia would have liked her very much.

On my side of the aisle are our newest business partners, the men of Volkov Industries. Adrik Volkov sits front and center with his wife and teenage daughter. His wife is holding their youngest on her lap.

Behind them are his brother, Marat Volkov, and his family. Followed by Josef Aziz, the head of Sigma

International, who I have known for years. And next to him are Andres Ramirez and his wife and children.

They are a huge fucking family, and I am not sure if they are necessarily my friends yet. But Nico and Adrik hit it off like birds of a feather after their first meeting.

After lending aid when my Koukla was in trouble, I figured inviting them was good business. And who knows? Maybe we can all be friends in the end.

Giselle seems to think it's a good idea, and I know enough to listen when my woman talks. Adrik nods his head at me.

I watch as he turns to say something to his wife, and she smiles brightly at him. They are still so in love after years of marriage and my chest squeezes.

I want that. With Giselle. I want it so fucking bad I can taste it. She told me she loved me the day of the rescue, and she's said it every day since. But I can't get enough of hearing it.

She is so perfect. I can't believe she's mine.

My Koukla.

But then the organ plays, and my attention is diverted to the back of the church.

One by one, the wedding party walks down the

aisle. Everyone is smiling, and the girls look teary-eyed. I can't smile back.

I'm too nervous.

There is a pause in the proceedings, and I frown.

Where is she?

I make a move to go look for her, but Nico has his hand on my shoulder.

"Easy," he whispers.

I'm glad he has a grip on me, cause that's when I see her, and I swear I almost fall down on my fucking knees.

This woman.

Giselle is wearing a strapless ballgown, and she looks like a princess in a fairytale.

She's beautiful. Breathtaking. She sparkles from head to toe.

Her hair is pulled back from her face with lacy little combs, allowing me a perfect view of her smooth skin and those gorgeous eyes of hers. But it's that mouth that has me meeting her at the bottom of the stairs, drawing me in.

She's wearing gloss. It's nice, but I like her better bare and she knows it.

Her eyes dance with mischief as her parents step back, grinning at us when I take Giselle's hand and pull her towards me, claiming her lips in a kiss I know shouldn't happen just yet.

But I'm Angel Fury and I don't follow the same rules as other people. And because she's mine, my Koukla doesn't push me away, she pulls me closer, opening her lips for me, and claims me back in front of everyone right then and there.

And it feels fucking divine. Like this is why I was born. To be hers.

"Excuse me? Guys, we need to do the ceremony first," Preacher butts in, but I don't stop kissing my bride until I am ready.

"You ready?" she asks, and I know her pretty smile is all for me.

"I love you, Koukla. I've been ready for this since the moment I saw you."

EPILOGUE-TWO-GISELLE

Marrying the man of my dreams with all our friends and family surrounding us has got to be the best thing that's ever happened to me.

Okay. Top two.

I'm panting, trying to catch my breath as my husband finally lifts his head from the cradle of my thighs where he just licked me to my first of what I hope is many orgasms.

"Goddamn. You taste even better now that we're married, Wife."

"Jesus, Angel. What a thing to say," I reply, biting my lip.

"You feel so soft. I love you," he tells me again, and my heart leaps inside my chest.

I never thought he would say it. Not even after I

confessed I loved him first, the day he rescued me from Ghost's clutches.

But he did say it. Out loud. In front of everyone. Right before we made our vows to each other. And he hasn't stopped saying it since.

I love it when he says he loves me.

"Good. Because I plan on saying it often, my Koukla," he says, nipping the soft skin on my belly.

Angel kisses and licks his way up my body, over my breasts, to my neck, and all the way up to my mouth. I feel his cock. His thick head stops right at my entrance. He is so close, he is teasing my dripping slit, but he does not penetrate me.

"Look at me, Koukla," he demands, lifting his body so I can see where we are almost joined.

I bite my lip, flexing my hips, but he moves with me.

"Watch with me. Watch as I make you part of me," he says, and fuck, it sounds so damn sexy.

Angel inches forward, and I arch my back. He is going slow.

So achingly slow.

But it feels so good. Like so much more than sex. It's like he is reaching deep into my soul, taking it, making it his.

And more than that, he is giving me his soul in

return. And every inch of him that pushes inside me is marking me, branding me as his.

Angel is so big. So surprisingly tender.

"That's it, Little Doll. Take me. Take. All. Of. Me."

He withdraws and pushes back in hard and deep. So deep.

"Angel. My Angel!"

I gasp and clutch at his sides. I adore his body. Angel is magnificent, and he loves me so perfectly.

His hands are everywhere. He is touching me all over. My thighs. My hips. Our chests pressed tightly together. He kisses me, too.

His tongue tangles with mine, and I am drunk on him. Next, he is wrapping his arms around my back, hugging me to him. Angel groans and fucks me harder.

His hips are pumping, the staccato bringing me higher and higher.

This is not the tender lovemaking I imagined on my wedding night when I was a little girl.

This is frenzied. Brutish. And everything I need.

He is everything. All I will ever need.

Angel's thighs push against mine, opening my legs farther, until the stretch is burning. But I love it. I want more.

He ruts into me at a punishing pace and before I

can even register it is happening, I am flying. Pure pleasure crashes into me like a tidal wave.

"Fuck, I love you," he growls, arching above me as he fills me with his cum, and he looks so perfect.

Like a god. Like an avenging angel.

I'm too spent to smile when he crushes me beneath his weight, trying to catch his breath. But I never felt complete happiness like I do in this moment. And it is all because of him.

My husband.

My Angel.

EPILOGUE THREE-NICO

"Well?" Angel asks as I step out of my wife's hospital room.

I accept the bag of clean clothes from him, knowing I am covered in all matter of biological stuffs. But I don't care.

I am riding high on the birth of Anna's and my second child.

"It's a girl," I announce, and the room breaks out into applause and well wishes.

All the leaders of the Vipers are there. Luc and Angel, my blood brothers, and their families. Our business partners from Volkov Industries, and our friends, are there as well.

I wasn't sure about that, but when the wives started insisting they come to support Anna, who has been welcomed along with Maria and Giselle into their circle of friends, well, there was nothing any of us could do.

The four wolves of Volkov Industries were just as unhinged and fucked in the head over their wives as we were.

"Congrats, brother," Angel says, and I nod, turning to get changed so I can rejoin my wife and child.

"Come here, Big Boy. Gonna meet your little sister when Daddy gets back from the bathroom," I tell my son who is sitting in his Aunt Sisi's lap.

"He can't wait," she says, and I nod.

My chest feels so damn full, and I take one more look at everyone around me, around us. I never thought I would have anything but darkness in my life.

But Anna brought me sunshine. She brought me soft things. Like flowers and butterfly kisses from my children.

She gives me everything and like the other men in the room, there is nothing I won't do for her.

Anna wanted family, and here we are. This is all for her.

My wife. The mother of my children. The very beat of my heart.

I get why Angel was so distracted when Sisi left town. It happened to me too, albeit not in the same way. And I know why Luc went nuts when someone went after Maria.

And from the stories I've heard about Adrik and his boys, well, it seems we are all cut from the same cloth.

We're not perfect. Hell, we ain't even good guys.

But we have one thing in common. One simple thing.

You touch our wives, you fucking die. Period.

Vipers don't pull their punches. We strike hard.

Don't believe me? Ask around. See how many of our enemies tried and lived to tell the tale.

Sure, we're mostly legitimate now. But as Angel always says, old habits die hard.

We don't shy from killing.

Not when it's necessary.

But to be honest, I'd much rather spend my time lovin' on my wife. And I am fairly certain Luc and Angel feel the same about their wives.

So, if you are thinking about stepping to us, if you have some notion you're a badass and can get away with fucking with us or our women, here is some free advice to ensure you live a long and healthy life.

Don't.

Just fucking don't.

Consider it a precautionary warning.

See, whatever you've heard, you got it wrong. The Vipers aren't weak because we're married.

Falling in love isn't a weakness at all.

It's the opposite. It makes us stronger than ever. And listening to me when I say *don't you fucking do it*, well, that just might save your life.

The end.

Did you enjoy this book? Please consider leaving a review so others can enjoy it.
Get all three Jersey Bad Boys in ebook, paperback, and discreet cover edition paperbacks today!
Thank you so much for your support.
xoxo, C.D. Gorri

HAVE YOU READ THE WILD BILLIONAIRE ROMANCE SERIES BY C.D. GORRI?

These wild billionaire playboys are used to getting their way…

There isn't much money can't buy, especially when it comes to pleasure. But can these curvy women tame these billionaire beasts and win their love? Or will their souls be sucked into oblivion by the wanton bliss their bodies crave more and more with every surrender?

Each of our heroes wears a mask on the outside to face the world, but his disguise comes off when he runs into the one female who makes his blood run hot. Need and possessive passion abound in these books, but our heroes know only one way to control their desires.

Will they f*ck the feeling they see as weakness out of

their systems, or will their needs only grow more wild with every touch, kiss, and plunge into ecstasy with the object of his affections?

Our Billionaire Heroes

Adrik Volkov
Marat Volkov
Josef Aziz
Andres Ramirez

Content Warnings

This series has profanity, graphic, steamy scenes, violence, homicide, talk of deceased relatives, references to sexual assault and abuse (not by the MCs), mention of domestic violence (not perpetrated by MCs), mention of suicide, alcohol consumption, misogyny (not the MCs), questionable morals, hurtful past, manipulations, fake relationships, lies, revenge, forced marriages, very bad decisions, and romantic obsessions that may be unhealthy. The FMC works at a shelter for abused women and children.
This is a fictional story with fictional characters. This is not real life.
*Always take care of your mental, emotional, and physical self because you are important.

P.S.

For those who asked Adrik is pronounced Ade-drick and Marat is Meh-Rut. Happy reading!

(PLEASE SUPPORT MY WILD BILLIONAIRE ROMANCE KICKSTARTER TODAY >>> https://www.kickstarter.com/projects/cdgorri/wild-billionaire-romance-audiobook-kickstarter)

WANT SHORT AND STEAMY ROMANCE? TRY THE CHERRY ON TOP TALES!

Do you love spicy romance with sizzling encounters, insta love, and passionate romances you can read in a couple of hours?

Full steam contemporary romance short stories where love is just the cherry on top?

Then Cherry On Top Tales are for you!

Get your copy today. This series is so hot, you'll never want the stories to end.

Her Yule His Log
His Carrot Her Muffin
Her Chocolate His Bar
His Pickle Her Jam

ALSO BY C.D. GORRI

Contemporary Romance Books:

Cherry On Top Tales

Her Yule His Log

His Carrot Her Muffin

Her Chocolate His Bar

His Pickle Her Jam

Wild Billionaire Romance

His Wild Obsession

His Wild Temptation

His Wild Seduction

His Wild Attraction

Jersey Bad Boys

Merciful Lies

Devious Lies

Pitiful Lies

***

Paranormal Romance Books:

Macconwood Pack Novel Series:

Macconwood Pack Tales Series:

The Falk Clan Tales:

The Bear Claw Tales:

The Barvale Clan Tales:

Barvale Holiday Tales:

Purely Paranormal Romance Books:

The Wardens of Terra:

The Maverick Pride Tales:

Dire Wolf Mates:

Wyvern Protection Unit:

Jersey Sure Shifters/EveL Worlds:

The Guardians of Chaos:

Twice Mated Tales

Hearts of Stone Series

Moongate Island Tales

Mated in Hope Falls

Speed Dating with the Denizens of the Underworld

Hungry Fur Love

Island Stripe Pride

NYC Shifter Tales

A Howlin' Good Fairytale Retelling

Witch Shifter Clan

Young Adult/Urban Fantasy Books

The Grazi Kelly Novel Series

<u>The Angela Tanner Files</u>

<u>G'Witches Magical Mysteries Series</u>

Co-written with P. Mattern

<u>Witches of Westwood Academy</u>

with Gina Kincade

<u>Blackthorn Academy For Supernaturals</u>

<u>*Be sure to check out my BUY DIRECT BUNDLES</u> and get 30% off when you buy available only my website.

Click here for The Official C.D. Gorri Reading List - free download

Coming Soon

Motley Crewd Shifters

Mergers & Acquisitions

ABOUT THE AUTHOR

USA Today Bestselling author C.D. Gorri writes paranormal and contemporary romance and urban fantasy books with plenty of steam and humor.

Join her mailing list here: https://www.cdgorri.com/newsletter

An avid reader with a profound love for books and literature, she is usually found with a book in hand. C.D. lives in her home state, New Jersey, where many of her characters and stories are based. Her tales are fast-paced yet detailed with satisfying conclusions. If you enjoy powerful heroines and loyal heroes who face relatable problems in supernatural settings, journey into the Grazi Kelly Universe today.

You will find sassy, curvy heroines and sexy, love-driven heroes who find their HEAs between the pages.

Wolves, Bears, Dragons, Tigers, Witches, Vampires, and tons more Shifters and supernatural creatures dwell within her paranormal works. The most important thing is every mate in this universe is fated, loyal, and true lovers always get their happily-ever-afters.

In her contemporary works, you will find fiercely possessive men and the smart, confident, curvy women they are crazy about. As always, the HEA is between the pages.

Thank you and happy reading!
del mare alla stella,
C.D. Gorri

http://www.cdgorri.com
https://www.facebook.com/Cdgorribooks
https://www.bookbub.com/authors/c-d-gorri
https://twitter.com/cgor22
https://instagram.com/cdgorri/
https://www.goodreads.com/cdgorri
https://www.tiktok.com/@cdgorriauthor

Milton Keynes UK
Ingram Content Group UK Ltd.
UKHW020047260824
447288UK00011B/295

9 781960 294630